ILLUM
DESP
ME4

MOVIE NOVEL

Andrews McMeel Publishing
a division of Andrews McMeel Universal
1130 Walnut Street, Kansas City, Missouri 64106

www.andrewsmcmeel.com

24 25 26 27 28 LAK 10 9 8 7 6 5 4 3 2 1

ISBN: 978-1-5248-8963-0

Library of Congress Control Number: 2024936197

Editor: Hannah Dussold
Designer: Marissa Asuncion
Production Editor: Brianna Westervelt
Production Manager: Chadd Keim

ATTENTION: SCHOOLS AND BUSINESSES
Andrews McMeel books are available at quantity discounts with
bulk purchase for educational, business, or sales promotional use.
For information, please e-mail the Andrews McMeel Publishing
Special Sales Department: sales@amuniversal.com.

ILLUMINATION'S DESPICABLE ME 4

MOVIE NOVEL

Adapted by Cala Spinner

Andrews McMeel
PUBLISHING®

CONTENTS

PROLOGUE

High in the skies on a picturesque European mountain sits a beautiful, ornate castle made of stone. This castle, of course, is no ordinary castle—it is a school. And this school is no ordinary school. It is the Lycée Pas Bon School of Villainy.

For centuries, the Lycée Pas Bon School of Villainy has seen powerful villains climb through its ranks. It imbued them with lessons of wrongdoing and then sent them on their way as graduates to complete their dastardly deeds. It is the alma mater of all of the great villains you've no doubt heard of, and maybe of some whose names you don't know yet.

And sometimes, of alumni who might surprise you.

CHAPTER 1

SCREEEEECH.

Gru's car came to a grinding halt. He parked and watched as his headlights turned off in the starry night. Then he stepped out of the vehicle and looked up. *There it was.* It felt like a lifetime ago that Gru had been enrolled there, at the Lycée Pas Bon School of Villainy.

POP! POP! SURPRISE! A mini sports car arrived, and three Minions—Phil, Ralph, and Ron—hopped out. They donned little suits and sunglasses, and they were ready for action.

"Okay, our target is Maxime Le Mal, one of the Anti-Villain League's most wanted," Gru instructed them. "There's no room for error, got it?"

The Minions nodded. "Si, boss!" they said in unison.

A flock of Lycée Pas Bon School of Villainy alumni headed toward the castle. They gathered together underneath a banner by the entrance that read: "WELCOME BACK CLASS OF '85".

It was showtime.

Gru and the Minions walked past the same welcome banner and entered the School of Villainy's grand hallway.

As the Minions sped off toward the buffet, Gru stood for a moment, taking it all in. There were villains to his right, left, and center. He moved through the crowd, passing through the seemingly endless thicket of outlaws, bandits, and villains, until—

"Hohoh!" One of the villains turned their attention toward Gru. "Well, well, well, look who it is." The voice had a heavy French accent, and it trilled with glee. "If it isn't *Gru-ser the Loser.* Hahaha!"

Bingo.

"Well, if it isn't Maxime Le Mal. You look . . ."

"Magnificent, yes, I know!" cut in Maxime. "What did you think, eh? That I was going to be a bald *loser* like you?"

"Well, that's not—"

"Ooooooh," the crowd hissed, seemingly in unison. They'd heard Maxime's burn. Even Ron and Ralph got caught up in the moment and "ooh"ed.

"It's good to laugh, no?" Maxime turned back to Gru. "Anyway, you remember my girlfriend, Valentina? She was captain of the Femmes Fatales Cheer Squad and the most popular girl in school, eh?"

Maxime gestured toward Valentina, who had a fluffy lapdog, Fifi, with her.

Of course Gru remembered her.

"Good to see you, Valentina," Gru said cordially to her. He mustn't get caught up in the moment—he had to stick to the plan.

Valentina scoffed. Then she flounced away, lapdog in tow.

Maxime laughed. "What happened, Gru? All your dreams of being a famous villain, they go poof-poof, eh?"

Gru straightened up a bit to defend himself.

"Well, I don't know if you know, but I did manage to steal the moon," Gru said, puffing up his chest.

"Really?" Maxime asked. "You mean *that* moon?" He pointed up at the castle's skylight looming over them. Sure enough, a bright, full moon could be seen shining through the opening. It was very much *not* stolen.

TAP. TAP. A noise reverberated throughout the crowd. That only meant one thing.

A small, elderly woman in a wheelchair was tapping the microphone on the stage of the castle's sweeping auditorium. "Can I have everyone's attention, please?" she said, and although it sounded like a question, Gru and the rest of the alumni knew it was a command. They all refocused their attention on her. This woman was Principal Ubelschlecht, and the villains knew better than to disobey her.

Once she was sure she had everyone's attention, Principal Ubelschlecht kicked things off. "Good evening and welcome!" she said.

"Wahoo!" some of the alumni cheered, but their voices were soon drowned out by a loud fanfare that played throughout the auditorium, welcoming everyone to the school's reunion.

As the music lulled, Principal Ubelschlecht added, "Now we are going to kick off the festivities by announcing the winner of our most coveted award—the Golden Alumni." She held up a golden statuette, and the crowd cheered again.

Principal Ubelschlecht commanded the mic again. "And so, without further ado . . ."

The crowd tensed.

". . . the winner of this year's Golden Alumni award is . . . uh . . ." Principal Ubelschlecht squinted at the paper revealing the award winner. "Oh!" A wicked grin spread across her face. "My favorite student . . ."

Gru braced himself.

"*Maxime Le Mal!*"

The crowd cheered loudly, and Gru caught sight of Maxime's gloating face relishing in his win.

"Oh, thank you, thank you. Merci," Maxime said to the crowd as he made his way to the stage to join Principal Ubelschlecht. "Merci beaucoup."

Gru raised his eyebrows.

Maxime took the stage.

"I'm sure you all know I have something very big in ze works," Maxime said into the mic. "Now, some of you laughed at my childhood obsession with cockroaches, but I quickly learned that they are a miracle of evolution."

As Maxime spoke, a roach crawled out of his sleeve. There were a few gasps from the crowd. Maxime ignored them.

"And I have found a way to harness the strength and the speed and . . . what is the word . . . *unsquishability* . . . of the most powerful creature on the planet," Maxime announced. "Which makes *me* . . . indestructible and unstoppable!"

The crowd seemed to be over their temporary disgust of Maxime's cockroach, because now they were cheering louder than ever.

"Maxime! Maxime! Maxime!" their voices echoed, blurring together into a chant for the school's newest Golden Alumni recipient.

"Behold," Maxime announced, "the power of the cockroach!"

With that, Maxime's entire body began to shake until it took the form of something half-human, half-roach.

SHROOP! Phil and Ron whipped out a flyswatter and some bug spray.

Maxime—still in the form of half a man, half a roach—was cackling, and the crowd was *loving it*, continuing to erupt in whoops and cheers.

Ralph got so caught up in the excitement that he tore his own overalls.

ZURP! Ron doused him with the bug spray.

"Stoppa!" Ralph said.

WHACK! The flyswatter came down on Ralph.

ZURP!! Ron doused him with the bug spray again.

"So, my sad little friend, what do you say about that, eh?" Maxime asked, this time focusing back on his old nemesis, Gru.

Now was Gru's chance to strike.

"Weeeeeeelllllllll," Gru started off. "I'd say you're . . ."—he paused for dramatic effect—"under arrest, courtesy of the Anti-Villain League!" Then Gru whipped out his Anti-Villain League badge.

Maxime chuckled. "Oh, hohoh! I don't think so, mon ami."

"Oh yeah?" It was Gru's turn to chide his old classmate. He pulled out the blaster from his jacket. He was quite sure that would be the end of their little tête-à-tête.

Only it wasn't.

Then Gru fired the Goop Grenade, which encased Maxime's roach body mid-leg, and Maxime, no doubt harnessing the power of the indestructible cockroach, broke free.

Gru aimed again, this time with another attack. But Maxime neutralized the blast before it reached him.

This was proving to be a tricky case. The two former classmates fought in seemingly endless swipes. Gru activated his watch communicator. He'd need to call in for backup.

"MOVE IN!" he yelped into the comm.

DING! CRAAAASH! WHOOP! At Gru's command, a legion of Anti-Villain League agents smashed through the windows of the castle.

"Anti-Villain League! Everybody, move, move, move!"

The AVL agents swarmed Maxime, surrounding him. Gru used one of their most powerful tools—an iron net— to ensnare Maxime in its clutches.

Gru breathed a sigh of relief. It was game over; the iron net was foolproof. The AVL had done it.

"Gotcha," Gru said.

"No, no, no, no, no, no, no, no," Maxime sneered back. "C'est impossible!"

But it *was* possible. Maxime was trapped within the net. As the AVL agents hauled him off and Valentina and Fifi slipped away, Gru could practically see the humiliation written all over his childhood archnemesis's face.

"GET YOUR HANDS OFF ME!" Maxime sneered at the AVL agents. "I AM COMMANDING YOU TO LET—"

Gru smiled. He'd waited decades for this moment—to see Maxime Le Mal *lose*, not just anywhere, but here, in these very halls.

He picked up the Golden Alumni award that Maxime had left behind in the onslaught. Long ago, this award had meant a lot to Gru. Now that it was in his grasp, it felt as good as he'd always dreamed it would. Perhaps even more so.

"So long, Maxime!" It was now Gru's turn to chide his rival, and he took upon this role dutifully. "Who's the loser now?"

"Loser! Loser! Loser!" chimed the Minions.

RIIIIIP! Maxime broke free from the net and charged at Gru. It looked like Maxime was going to win, but then the AVL agents subdued him.

"This is not over!" Maxime wailed at Gru. "You won't always have the AVL to fight your battles, you coward! I will *exterminate* you!"

But his voice got quieter and quieter as he screamed, for the AVL agents were dragging him away.

While Maxime's screaming tapered off, Gru inspected a small cut where Maxime had nicked him just before the AVL agents intervened. Still, a simple cut was a small price to pay for finally getting back at Maxime Le Mal.

And then . . . **CLANG!**

The head of the Golden Alumni award toppled off. Gru shivered.

CHAPTER 2

When Gru wasn't on AVL missions, he was just a simple man trying to support his family. One afternoon, Gru arrived at home, carrying quite a few bags filled with groceries.

"Hello, everybody!" Gru called out to his family.

Margo, Edith, and Agnes were seated at the kitchen counter. They perked their heads up and said hello to Gru with choruses of "Hey, Gru!" and "I'm so happy you're here!"

The youngest of the girls, Agnes, leapt out of her seat and neared Gru. With her was Lucky, a small goat. Agnes had once said that Lucky was "the best goat in the whole wide world."

"Look what I taught Lucky," she said proudly. "Lucky, *sit!*"

Lucky stared at her.

He most definitely did not sit.

And then he *pooped*.

"Ah, Lucky! I said *SIT*," Agnes tried again.

Lucky licked her face. This got a laugh from Agnes, at least, and she hugged him back.

Gru turned to put the groceries away, but not before telling Agnes, "Uh, maybe we practice *outside* from now on."

Then Lucy, Gru's wife, entered the room.

"There's my husband! Did you remember to get the milk?" she asked.

Gru eyed the many different milk jugs as he pulled them out of the shopping bag.

"Well, yes," he said. "They had a few kinds." He hadn't been sure *which* milk to buy, so he'd bought them all—almond, soy, hemp, oat, goat, chocolate, half-and-half, powdered, and milk of magnesia.

"What about regular milk?" Lucy asked him.

"They don't make that anymore," Gru replied. "Wait a minute!" He looked at the three girls and playfully counted them. "One, two, three girls," he said. Then he looked back at Lucy. "One wife." He looked around again. "Something is missing . . ."

"No, I think that's all of us, yeah?" Lucy replied. Then she said, "You know what I keep forgetting? THIS GUY!"

Lucy turned slightly to reveal a baby strapped onto her back. He was securely fastened in a carrier.

"There's my boy. There he is!" Gru said, giddy. "A coochie-coo. Where is Daddy's hug?"

But the baby, who had seemed perfectly happy moments before Gru spoke to him, now had a look of disdain. The baby slapped his pacifier out of his own mouth.

"Ooh, looks like somebody's a little cranky. Behind that sourpuss, I know you love your dada. Go on, say 'dada.' Daaaaaaa—" Gru reached out to move the baby's lips.

"Of course he loves you, he just doesn't show it on his face," Lucy said. "Or with his body language." Then she faced the baby. "Gru Jr., come on. Show Daddy how much you love him."

Gru Jr.'s face switched from joy at his mama Lucy to a frown at Gru.

Gru had a new idea. "Oh, I know what will make you happy!" Gru said. He reached into one of the grocery bags and pulled out a tube of squeezable baby food. "Mmm. Bahama Medley!"

Gru opened the cap of the squeezable food and offered it to the baby, but he turned his head away and cried.

WAAAA! WAAAA! WAAAAAAA!

"No? It's from the Bahamas! All of them!" Gru said, trying to tempt Jr. into eating it. "Mmm, mmmm, mmmm!"

In a last, desperate move, Gru tasted the baby food himself.

"That really tastes like the Bahamas!" Gru noted, surprised.

This seemed to work—the baby saw the tube in Gru's mouth and his eyes seemed to light up. He reached out and squeezed it.

SPLURT! The baby food shot out of Gru's nostrils and mouth and splattered onto his shirt.

"That really tastes like the Bahamas." Gru's eyes were watering. The baby laughed and rubbed the food goo on his bald head.

"See? He loves his daddy. He's *sharing*," Lucy said to Gru.

Gru held Jr. away from his body—and his messy shirt—while the baby continued laughing.

"Phil, Ralph, Ron!" Gru hissed.

At his command, the three Minions, dressed like a pit crew team, rolled into the kitchen with a cart full of supplies. Like they were working at NASCAR, they took the baby, cleaned his face, tickled his feet, changed his diaper, brushed his hair, replaced his pacifier, and quickly handed the baby back to Gru, complete with an air freshener on the baby's foot.

"Thanks, guys," Gru said to them.

DING DONG. The doorbell sounded, and the Minions raced away to answer it. At the door was none other than Silas Ramsbottom, the head of the Anti-Villain League. He was looking rather grim.

"Ramsbottom?" Gru said out loud.

"Hehe." The Minions giggled. Gru had said "bottom."

Silas entered the house and faced Lucy and Gru.

"I need a word with you both," he said to them. "I'm sorry, but there is no time for chitchat!" He took out his laptop and faced Gru. "Maxime Le Mal has sent you a message from prison."

Gru and Lucy looked at Silas's laptop, where a video from an incarcerated (and still part-roach) Maxime Le Mal was loading.

"Bonjour, Gru!" Maxime said into the security camera. "I know you can hear me, so hear this! You think you can humiliate me and get away with it, yes? But no! When I break out of prison, I'm coming for my revenge, Gru! But this time, I won't go so easy on you! Ha, ha, ha!" As if invigorated by the laughter, Maxime broke out of his restraints. "And," he sung, as he grabbed the security camera with his spindly roach arms, "I know where you live! So you'd better sleep with one eye open, 'cuz you can't hide from me. Hahahaha! Sweet dreams, Gru-ser."

One more laugh from Maxime, and then he crushed the camera.

Gru and Lucy gasped. Gru was terrified, but he didn't want to show it, so he put on a brave face.

"Don't worry," he said to Lucy. "He can't get out of there. It's a maximum security prison."

"Ah, yes," Silas murmured. "Well. Um." He looked even more grim than when he'd entered the house. "He escaped yesterday."

"WHAT?" Now Gru couldn't contain himself. This was cause for alarm. If Maxime Le Mal knew where Gru and his family lived . . . then they weren't safe.

And they had to move. *Fast.*

Silas had just the plan.

"Leave our home?!" Agnes said, shocked, when they told her the news. Gru and Lucy were helping the girls pack their suitcases.

"You're gonna love it," Gru said, trying his best to sound chipper. "It's—it's called the safe house, and it's fun and it's safe and it's fantastic and we're going."

Lucy followed his lead. "Yeah, you'll get a new room, go to a new school. That'll be fun, right? Everything's gonna be new! We love new!"

"What about all my friends?" asked Margo.

ZIP! Gru closed up some luggage.

"You'll make new friends. Probably better ones."

Margo's eyes went wide. She didn't want to move. She flopped onto a piece of furniture.

"Ugh. I can't believe this," she moaned, full of teenage angst.

"Yes, yes, lots of emotions. Big life change. Less talking. More walking. Come on. Here we go," Gru said. He ushered everyone toward the door. The family was loaded up with suitcases.

Lucy, holding Gru Jr., exited the house with Gru, Agnes, Margo, Edith, Phil, Ralph, and Ron, each carrying some items. Agnes was the last to leave. She sniffled at the bottom of the steps and faced Lucky. She held on to his leash as an AVL agent walked behind her with Kyle, Gru's "dog," in a carrier.

"I'm sorry you can't go with us, Lucky," Agnes said to the goat.

BLEEEEEAT.

Lucy wrapped her arms around the goat and hugged him tight. Then she gave his leash to the AVL agent.

"Take good care of him," she said to the agent and then turned to Lucky. "Be good, Lucky! Don't forget to practice your tricks." She watched as the AVL agent and Lucky walked away.

Gru watched this farewell sadly. He felt awful. He never wanted it to come to this. But he needed to keep them safe.

SLAM! The door shut as the family gathered into a large car. The girls looked out the window, watching the house they loved get smaller and smaller as the car pulled away from their old life and into their new one.

A few moments later, Silas Ramsbottom piped up from the driver's seat.

"We'll arrive at the AVL safe house in a few hours. Mayflower is a lovely town. A lovely, safe, boring town. Trust me; it is for the best, Gru."

Agnes leaned forward.

"And what about Grandma? And Uncle Dru?"

"I'm sorry. NO ONE can know of your whereabouts. Not even family," Silas replied.

This, at least, got a smirk out of Gru.

"Bingo!" he said. "There's your silver lining."

"And you promise to take care of the other Minions?" Edith asked Silas.

"They'll be safe and sound at the AVL headquarters. I have big plans for them," Silas promised her.

Gru scoffed.

"Good luck with that," he said.

But Gru was wishing luck on the wrong person. He should've wished it on Carl the Bus Driver.

As Gru and his family ventured toward new horizons, a huge AVL bus rode down the highway.

Inside was total chaos. Minions were singing, dancing, bouncing from seat to seat, and throwing paper airplanes. At the front of the bus, Carl the Bus Driver was hit with a spitball.

"THAT IS IT!" roared Carl the Bus Driver.

SCREEEEEECH! The bus cut across a few lanes of traffic and came to a stop on the side of the road.

Carl the Bus Driver got out of his seat and faced the Minions. Bubbles floated everywhere, but he was furious.

"You are now on Carl's bus! And Carl is a longtime AVL employee whose retirement benefits are almost vested! So while on Carl's bus, you follow Carl's rules. No shenanigans. No antics. And NO tomfoolery!"

"Tom?" one Minion piped up.

The Minions were quiet for a moment. Carl meant business.

Carl wasn't having it. "This ends NOW. Or you're gonna see a side of Carl you do not want to see." He popped a nearby bubble seemingly with the fire in his eyes alone. "Do I make myself clear?"

For a moment, there was silence. And then . . .

"BAZOOKA!" yelled a Minion who wasn't listening.

SPLAT! Carl got pied in the face.

The bus descended into chaos once more.

And in case you were wondering, the Minions *did* end up arriving at the AVL headquarters . . .

But Carl wasn't the one driving the bus.

A Minion was.

When they arrived at the headquarters, the Minions carried a helpless Carl into the building and rode the elevators to the top.

CHAPTER 3

Silas drove the car through the town of Mayflower. All of the houses and lawns were neat and tidy and ... perfect.

"The safe house has been used to protect our agents for decades now," Silas said.

Margo looked out the window. "Are we really gonna live here?" she asked.

"Look at that fountain!" said Agnes.

"Awesome," Edith added.

The girls continued to gawk at the houses in the neighborhood while Phil snored in the backseat. Ralph tapped Ron.

"Hey, hey, looka," Ralph said to him.

While Phil continued to snooze, Ralph uncapped a marker and drew a pig snout on Phil's face.

"And here it is . . . your new home!" Silas announced.

Silas pulled to a stop in front of a simple house. It was smaller than the others that they had driven by, and it was quite unkempt with faded paint. But it was a house nonetheless.

"Oh," Lucy said.

Gru tried to be encouraging.

"I'm sure it's gonna be great!" he said. "Silas says that there's a pool in the back! That'll be fun, huh?"

Silas and the family entered via the front door and took in the safe house. Unbeknownst to them, a teenage girl was watching from the next door window, but they didn't notice. They looked around at the safe house's furnishings. It was decked out in AVL-issued furniture and looked like something out of 1992, but not in a cool, chic way—in a way that made it dated and old. It was filled with filing cabinets and office furniture. It looked more like a break room than a home.

Everyone's face fell. No one was impressed.

"Wow. It's so . . . cold and uninviting," Lucy said, but then tried to sound upbeat. "But in a homey kind of way." Still, her face couldn't hide her disappointment.

"Yes, everything here is AVL standard—a high-tech security bunker disguised as a home," Silas explained. "There's even a fully automated lockdown mode. Isn't that fun?" He gestured to a red button on the wall.

Agnes spotted the vending machine and brightened up.

"It has a vending machine!" she said. "I LOVE this place!!!"

The Minions decided to check out the vending machine themselves.

Ralph ran and got his head stuck in the vending machine headfirst, which left his butt exposed outside the machine.

Ron and Phil took turns slapping Ralph's butt.

SLAP!

SLAP!

SLAP!

Silas gestured to a folder he was holding.

"Alright, now down to business. For your own safety, you'll all be assuming new identities."

"New identities?" asked Gru. "Is that really necessary?"

Silas was stern. "It's not up for debate," he replied. Then he took out some papers and faced Gru. "Now, you are a solar panel salesman." He turned to Lucy. "You're a hair stylist at an upscale salon."

"A hair stylist? Yes! Jackpot! Silas, did you choose that because you know that I cut my own hair and that I would totally rock at this?" Lucy asked him.

Silas blinked back at her.

"No," he said.

Gru looked down at his paper. "*Chet Cunningham*," he read out loud. "Yeah, that's got a nice ring to it."

Edith read her paper. Her name was now Blair.

Agnes read hers.

"Britney?" she asked.

Margo scowled, looking at her own new identity. "My name is Bree?!"

"Oh, come on. There are worse names than Bree," Lucy said to her.

"Yeah, like Blanche," Margo replied.

Lucy laughed.

"Oh, that is a terrible name. Imagine being named Blanche. Truly I cannot think of a worse . . ." Lucy then saw Margo's smirking face. "My name's Blanche, isn't it?"

Margo smiled. "Yup," she said.

The girls giggled.

"Well, I'll get used to it," Lucy sighed.

Silas stepped forward and clapped his hands. He told the girls to go pick out their rooms while he spoke with their parents.

The girls bounded up the stairs, and the Minions followed them eagerly, leaving Ralph stuck *inside* of the vending machine.

Silas led Lucy, Gru, and Gru Jr. to the front door. He had something else to say.

"I didn't want to frighten the girls, but it is absolutely crucial that you keep your true identities under wraps. Gru, you're going to have to try to not be so . . . Gru-ish."

"What is that supposed to mean?" asked Gru.

"Well, I'm just saying, you tend to stand out in a crowd, that's all," Silas replied. "You know, you—like the way you're always cranky and irritable . . . and, uh, how you make things a bit awkward for everyone around you."

"You *do* do that. I mean, you know you—" Lucy chimed in, hoping to grant Silas a save.

"I don't make people awkward or uncomfortable! I'm VERY comforting! Like a nice meatloaf! I'm pretty delicious." Gru was agitated. Silas and Lucy stared at him, hoping he would realize the awkward moment he just created. "This is not awkward! *You're* the ones who are making it awkward!"

"Gru, you *have* to blend in. Your family's lives are at stake. You understand?" Silas said.

Gru Jr. happily babbled while in Lucy's arms.

"Of course, yes. Fully understand," Lucy answered for her husband. "We would do anything to keep our family safe."

"Right, well, I'll be in contact when this is all over. Until then, capturing Maxime Le Mal is our top priority." He opened the door and looked both ways. "Stay safe." Then he left without saying another word.

Lucy and Gru turned to each other. Gru looked uneasy, but Lucy tried to reassure him.

"You know what, Gru? Maybe this isn't so bad. We need a break from chasing down villains and dangerous missions, right? We can actually be a normal family for once—"

Gru was simmering down. "And I can finally spend some real bonding time with the baby," he said. He faced Gru Jr. "It's gonna be great . . . right, pal?" He leaned toward him. "Who's got your nose? Who's got your—"

The baby latched on to Gru's nose with both of his hands and pulled.

"Ah! He's got my nose!" Gru shouted. He pulled free and attempted to play it off. "Quite the grip there. That kid is strong."

CHAPTER 4

A cockroach climbed out of a city garbage truck and slipped into a sewer drain. He fell all the way through until he finally landed in an underground tunnel.

He slipped through a grate. Made his way lower. And then he arrived . . . in Maxime Le Mal's underground lair. With Maxime Le Mal, freshly broken out of prison.

It was a huge celebration. Maxime and Valentina, along with a crowd of cockroaches, were dancing. Maxime and Valentina walked down a red carpet that the cockroaches unfurled in front of them. A banner behind them read: "WELCOME HOME, MAXIME!"

"Ah, haha! Thank you! Look at everyone, yes? We are having a good time, right?" Maxime addressed the crowd.

He blew kisses and finished with a flourish. "Thank you, my beautiful army! Maxime's back, baby! Ha, ha, ha, HA!"

The roaches danced and cheered.

"And a special *merci beaucoup* to everyone who helped me break out of AVL prison." Maxime gestured to the crowd. "Todd and Linda, where are you?" He wanted to recognize them for distracting the guards. Todd and Linda waved and then chest bumped each other.

But then Maxime's demeanor changed. It was time to be serious.

"Now, silence. We must make Gru suffer for arresting me," he commanded. "And what better way than to take away from him . . . his *precious little baby*!" Maxime gestured to a projector screen where a giant drawing of Gru Jr. appeared. He wanted to steal that baby very badly.

Valentina stepped forward and opened her mouth. "Oh, Maxime—"

"No, no! Wait, wait. Not *Maxime*. What if I start going by . . . COCKROACH MAN?" Maxime put a lot of effort into attempting to convince her on this. "Huh? Little on the nose but it is very clear, eh? It's good, no?"

"Ay, I am not calling you that stupid name," Valentina replied. Then her face lit up. "But I LOVE this evil plan!"

"Well, he has it coming," Maxime replied, talking about Gru. "He humiliated me in front of the whole school. I had my trophy and everything! But now, ze game begins."

CHAPTER 5

The next morning, Ron and Phil were enjoying floaties in the pool outside the safe house.

POW! Ron slapped Phil with a pool noodle.

Ralph watched them play from his position inside of the vending machine, which was now outside. Within its glass walls, he was wearing a one-eyed goggle and a snorkel, hoping to join in on the fun.

Meanwhile, Gru and Lucy made breakfast in the kitchen.

"Okay, we've got Chet's famous super cheesy scrambled eggs, and Blanche's famous bacon that spells your name," Gru intoned, acting out his new role.

He served Agnes her plate and spun it around. The name "BRITNEY" was spelled out in bacon.

Agnes frowned. She realized what she would have to do.

"Wait, I can't say my name is Britney. That would be a lie," she said.

"Yes," replied Gru.

"But we aren't supposed to lie," said Agnes.

"Don't think of it as lying. Think of it as high-stakes pretending," Gru corrected her.

Agnes shook her head. "Well, I'm not going to," she said.

"Ah, just a little white lie?" Gru nudged.

"Nope." Agnes folded her arms.

"Agnes! As your father, I command you to lie."

"No."

"Yes! Lie!"

Agnes shook her head again. "Mm-mm."

"You are walking on thin ice, little lady!"

Agnes stared down at her plate. She was holding her ground. As she did so, Gru Jr. reached over and stole a piece of crispy bacon off her fork.

Gru looked around for backup. Edith was eating her breakfast.

"Why can't you be more like your sister Edith? She lies all the time!"

"No, I don't," Edith replied.

"See?" Gru said. "See?! She's lying right now. Beautifully, I might add."

Lucy stepped in.

"Okay, you guys. This is our first big day in Mayflower, and I say we make it a great one." She walked over to Agnes and Gru Jr. and squeezed their shoulders. "Right, Chet Jr.?" She raised the baby over her head. The baby giggled in reply.

CHIME! A clock sounded.

"We're gonna be late for karate!" Edith said.

Lucy turned to Gru. "And you have to get Margo to school."

The girls ran off to get ready.

Lucy could tell that Gru was feeling defeated already, and the day hadn't even begun.

"Hey," she said in a soothing voice. "You just have to put yourself out there, and I promise, Mayflower will love Chet Cunningham." She kissed him on the cheek and then handed him the baby. "And you, little man," she said, facing the baby, "are gonna have so much fun with your daddy today!" She blew them both kisses.

Gru looked down at Gru Jr.

"Yup. Just you and Dada. Come on, say it. . . . Dada! Daaaaa-daaaaa!"

The baby started to open his mouth as if he was about to attempt it. Gru leaned in hopefully. Then the baby blew a raspberry in his face.

Gru frowned.

Later, Gru stepped out of the front door, ready for his big first day. He was dressed in his Mayflower best—a pink polo shirt and khaki pants. Margo was behind him, followed by the Minions, who were back in their pit crew uniforms and were carrying Gru Jr. in his car seat. They walked toward the minivan and loaded the baby inside using a drill to secure the car seat.

Gru saw that their next-door neighbor was *also* heading out for the morning.

"Look, Margo, neighbors," he said quietly to her. Then he puffed out his chest and turned to the neighbor. He was going to do his best to fit in, just like he'd promised. "Hello!" he said. He tried to convince himself that he could handle this, but he wasn't so sure. Then he grabbed the neighbor's hand and introduced himself. "I'm your new neighbor, Chet Cunningham."

The neighbor looked Gru over, unimpressed.

"Perry Prescott," the neighbor replied. "So, what, uh, brings you to the neighborhood, Chet?"

"Well, uh. . . ." Gru squirmed for a moment. This was a mission, just like the others. He couldn't mess this up! "Solar panels! That's it. I sell solar panels." Then he tried to collect himself. "Have you joined the solar revolution?"

"Uh, I think I'm good," Perry replied. He walked over to his car.

"Good to know," Gru said, as if they were still in the middle of their conversation. "So, wha—what do you do, Perry?"

"I own Prescott Motors, the largest auto dealer in the state," Perry replied.

"Wow, that's impressive," Gru said, unsure how to continue the conversation as he normally wasn't one for chitchat. But then he saw Margo walking over to them, so he introduced her, and accidentally forgot her new identity. "This is my daughter, Margo."

"*Bree*, Dad," Margo quickly corrected him.

Gru had to cover for his mistake.

"Ah! Yes, yes. Did I say Margo? It's funny because I was thinking—I was thinking about a fish I once had as a pet named Margo . . . who lived in the pond. And, uh, then died."

This was not going well.

"Anyway. I, uh, I am about to take Bree to school for her first day," Gru finished.

"Yeah, I was about to take Poppy to school," Perry replied. His own teenage daughter, Poppy, appeared in the driveway, but she didn't notice Gru or Margo—her eyes were glued to her phone. She'd seen them arrive last night, anyway, through the window.

"Poppy! Hello, Poppy. That's a fun name to say. You want to carpool with us?" Gru asked her.

Poppy made a face.

"No," she said.

"You can be friends with Bree!" He turned to Margo, "Right, Bree? You don't have any friends!"

Poppy glanced at Margo, shook her head, and got into her own dad's car.

"Well, love to chitchat, Chet, but she's got school," Perry started to say. "And I'm meeting some pals over at the country club, so—"

"Ooh, country club? That sounds like a lot of fun. If I were ever invited to a country club, I am sure that I would love it." Gru stared at Perry for a moment, hoping for an invitation. But it never came. Instead Perry said, "Yeah. Well, we really have to get going, so . . . nice meeting you, Chet!"

Then Perry and Poppy drove off. Gru waved as they did so. "Okay, cool! Any time you want to hang out, just hit me up with a text!" he called out.

Once the father-daughter neighbor duo were out of eyesight, Gru turned to Margo.

"That was painful," Margo told him.

Gru, Margo, and Gru Jr. drove through Mayflower to get to school.

"You'll see. By lunchtime, you will have forgotten all about your old, lousy friends," Gru told Margo.

"Mmm, not so sure about that," Margo replied.

Gru pulled up in front of the school and stopped the minivan. He looked over at Margo, who was clearly struggling to get out of the vehicle. He put a hand on her arm.

"Hey, honey. You got this. You are smart. You are funny. What's there to worry about, right? They're gonna love you!"

Margo smiled at Gru. She knew he was trying his best, even though he was still awkward.

"Thanks, Gru," she said. Then she stepped out of the minivan and headed into school. Gru sighed nervously and muttered to himself, "Oh, please let them love you . . ."

Then he turned to drive off when he saw Poppy in the crosswalk in front of him, staring. He smiled and waved at her, but she only glared further, until finally, the tips of her lips lifted into an odd smile.

"Er," Gru said out loud, totally unnerved. He watched as she crossed to the sidewalk.

BEEEEEP! The cars behind him were impatient.

"Move it!" bellowed a lady from her car.

"Sorry, my bad! I'm going, I'm going," Gru called out to her. He hit the gas and took off.

CHAPTER 6

Meanwhile, at the AVL headquarters, the Minions were up to their usual shenanigans and tomfoolery. A Minion was trying on X-ray glasses.

"Oooo, glasses! Oooo! Huh?" the Minion said.

As the Minion looked through the glasses, a group of other Minions walked by. And this Minion could see ... EVERYTHING!!! He could see their entire skeletons!

Another Minion came out and spooked the Minion with the X-ray glasses, and he fainted.

Meanwhile, another group of Minions was scaling a training wall. A Minion on the ground accidentally fired a grappling hook, which embedded itself into a climbing

Minion's clothing and pulled him back to th

This caused the entire wall to cascade downward t

Silas Ramsbottom and a group of AVL scientists

clipboards and lab coats walked past them, surveying

everything. Silas got the Minions' attention, and they all

lined up for him.

"Some of you may be wondering why you're here,"

Silas addressed them.

The Minions exchanged looks. One raised his hand.

Why *were* they there?

"We are looking for the strong . . . the mighty . . . the

fearless," Silas said. "We need the best of the best." This

was all part of a secret initiative to help stop Maxime Le

Mal. "So, who's it going to be?" Silas asked them.

All of the Minions behind the front row nervously

took a step backward, which made the front row look like

they had volunteered.

Silas smiled.

"Yes, nice work, gentlemen," he said to them.

The volunteered Minions were unhappy, and the rest

of the Minions laughed at them.

"The AVL is known for cutting-edge weapons and

vehicles . . . but now we are developing cutting-edge

AGENTS! And I can think of no better guinea pigs than you."

ents? This piqued the volunteered

y turned back to the other Minions

t them.

first to test our super-serum

you into elite agents with powers

abilities far beyond those of mortal man," Silas continued, and gestured behind him to high-tech individual pods. He walked to the controls. "Or you might just explode," he added quietly with a shrug. "We don't really know."

At that, the volunteered Minions' faces fell. But it was too late to back out now. Extender arms came out of the pods and dragged the Minions into them. Silas pressed some buttons and turned a dial on the control panel.

ZZZZAP! After he did so, a jolt of electricity hit the pods, and they vibrated with energy.

The Minions inside began to transform. . . .

SMASH! Mega Dave's fists came crashing through his pod. He easily ripped the machine that held him back just moments ago with his huge, bulging muscles. He now wielded the power of super strength.

A red laser beam emitted from the next pod over, which sliced it in three. In the middle of that pod was Mega Mel, and the red laser beam had come from none other than his eye. He struck a pose but was facing the wrong way. He quickly corrected himself. **KA-POW!**

A suuuuuuuper stretched out Mega Tim emerged from the next pod, but his foot got stuck in the pod's machinery. After a bit of tugging, he yanked it free and was propelled forward from the force of the tug. He was now a Minion of super stretchy ability.

The next pod had bite marks all over it, and Mega Jerry was eating his way out of the machine. He emerged from the contraption with a perfectly round, rock-solid body, and rolled forward like a boulder.

SLAM! SLAM! SLAM! In the last pod, there were three loud noises before Mega Gus burst out and floated up. Of the volunteers, it was clear that Mega Gus was the least in control of his new flying powers. His head was dented but then reformed in the shape of a cone.

The newly enhanced Minions struck a pose together.

Silas was very pleased they hadn't exploded.

"Ladies and gentlemen, I give you . . . The Mega Minions!"

CHAPTER 7

Lucy dropped Edith and Agnes off at karate class. They were each wearing a gi, the traditional uniform worn in karate.

"Aw, you guys look adorable. And really tough. And scary," Lucy told them.

"I'll look even better when I have a black belt. Hi-ya!" Edith said.

"Ooo! Ooo! I'm gonna break a brick with my HEAD," said Agnes.

"That's the spirit!" Lucy smiled.

GONG! Someone hit a gong, signaling the start of class.

"Okay, now go have fun while I'm at work," Lucy said, leaning in close to the girls.

"We will," Edith promised.

"Blair and Britney, right?"

"Mmm," Agnes replied nervously. She made a face. She wasn't happy about potentially having to lie but forced a smile back anyway. "Okay. Bye, Mom," she said.

Agnes and Edith took their places on the mat, along with the other kids.

Their instructor, Sensei O'Sullivan, turned to the class. He had bright, curly red hair and pale skin. He scowled at the room full of children and performed a karate move, as if trying to impress them—or perhaps to intimidate them.

"Hi-ya! Circle up, people," Sensei O'Sullivan said. "Show respect for your sensei!"

"Yes, Sensei O'Sullivan!" the children all shouted in unison. Then they knelt in a circle. "Hai!"

Sensei O'Sullivan walked to the center of the circle. There was a beat, and then Edith and Agnes knelt too. Sensei O'Sullivan pointed at a boy with shaggy hair.

"You, Moscovitch. Didn't I tell you to cut that hair? You look like a sheepdog," he said.

"Sorry, sensei," the boy replied timidly.

Edith and Agnes exchanged glances.

"Now, we have two new students today," Sensei O'Sullivan said. He asked Agnes to step forward and tell everyone her name.

Agnes gulped. This was exactly what she didn't want to do. She looked up at the instructor.

"Um," she said.

She glanced at Edith.

"It's Britney," Edith whispered to her.

Agnes just couldn't find it within herself to lie.

"Uh, m-my name? I can't . . ."

Sensei O'Sullivan was *not* pleased by this. "There's no *can't* in ka-ra-te!" he barked. "Ten push-ups after class."

Edith watched from the mat. She did *not* like how Sensei O'Sullivan was treating her sister. She stood up.

"Hey! That's not fair."

Sensei O'Sullivan cartwheeled over to Edith.

"You better not be talking back to your sensei," he chided. Then he returned to Agnes with no sign of softening. "Now, are you ready to tell us your name and participate?"

"Mmm, I guess not," Agnes replied.

This angered Sensei O'Sullivan. He wasn't above fighting children—and he decided to show off his moves. But Edith got the best of him—**CRUNCH!** She stomped on his foot! He fell back and slammed into the giant gong.

The other kids in class gasped. Edith bowed, and the kids cheered for her.

"That was for my sister," Edith told the sensei. She high-fived and hugged Agnes. Sensei O'Sullivan looked at his foot and whimpered, "You broke my PINKY TOE!" Agnes looked at Edith.

"That's gonna be a lot of push-ups," she said.

Lucy approached her station at the upscale Mane on Main Hair Salon.

"Oh, uh, Mrs. Cunningham!" called out the owner, a woman named Verna.

Lucy had almost forgotten that was her name. "Oh! Yeah, uh, yeah. Uh, hi," she said.

Verna smiled at her. She was excited that Blanche Cunningham was going to cut hair at the salon.

"Well, you are exactly what we need here," Verna said. Apparently there were a lot of vain, demanding divas in the town.

As if on cue, a well-dressed woman entered the salon. All eyes seemingly darted toward her. She flounced in like she owned the place.

"I have a hair emergency!" the woman wailed. "Where's what's-her-name? Remy? Rhonda?"

"Oh, Melora, I'm so sorry. Rachel's on maternity leave," Verna said to her.

"What?" the woman—Melora—barked.

Verna tried to placate her. "But you are in luck! Because Blanche here is fantastic." Verna gestured to Lucy, who smiled at Melora. But Melora didn't see that smile because she had already marched off to the private station, ready to get her hair serviced. Lucy laughed awkwardly to herself.

Lucy set Melora up and brushed her hair.

"So, what are we thinking?" she asked the woman. "What if we just wet the hair and let it dry in the air, let nature do its *thang*. You know?"

"No, no, no, no," Melora cut in. "This style is dead to me. It's time for a whole *new* Melora. I want *this*." She took out a photo on her phone of a completely different style of hair that seemed rather complicated and was a wild pink color.

Lucy's eyes widened.

"Wow. Heh. Wow. Uh. Okay. Let's start with color? Yes, color. 'Cause that's what you start with." Lucy muttered the last part under her breath.

She turned away to mix some dye and tried to figure out what to do as she went. She applied gobs of the dye to Melora's hair.

"A little of this . . . some of that . . ." Lucy poured more dye on Melora's head. "And, ooh. That's pretty. This isn't so hard!"

The dye, meanwhile, was bubbling in Melora's hair. Now what? Lucy refreshed the website on her phone, titled "Perfect Hair Color." Then she looked over at Melora and saw that the woman's hair was *smoking*!

"Should it be *smoking*?" Melora asked.

"Uh . . . smoking means it's working?" Lucy tried, though she wasn't totally sure what was happening.

Lucy used the hair color brush on Melora, but a clump of Melora's hair came out and onto the brush. Confused, Lucy held up the brush to inspect it. It combusted into flames.

Lucy threw the flaming brush into a bowl of water and it splashed up and onto the electric light bulbs at the private workstation. Sparks flew, and the light bulbs around them started to explode.

POP, POP, POP!

The scene caused an electrical short throughout the salon, and now *every* light bulb was exploding.

Verna panicked. "Call 911!"

Everyone inside the salon fled, and the overhead sprinklers embedded in the ceiling turned on, raining down on the entire store. Lucy darted out of the building with the crowd, but once outside, she sped off. She watched as fire trucks made their way over, no doubt ready to put out the fire.

Lucy picked up her pace. She was eager to leave. And she didn't want to know what had become of Melora's hair, but she was okay with never finding out.

"Voilà."

Maxime held up his masterpiece in celebration. He struck a pose.

"My latest creation! All of my transformation powers in a handheld design, eh?"

"Ay, I love it!" Valentina cried. "Oh! And look at the little antennae. That's so cute." She playfully flicked the roach antennae that adorned the Roachification Ray.

"It's not supposed to be cute, no," Maxime shot back. "I'm going for *intimidating*! Terrifying, even!"

Maxime pulled the ray away in frustration. "Now, all I have to do is find that walking baked potato and his baby is *mine*." There was a photo of Jr. on Maxime's projector.

But Maxime wasn't done showing off yet. He held up the remote again and said, "Check this out." Before them appeared a real, large aircraft. Fifi barked at it.

It was a giant, roach-shaped ship.

CHAPTER 8

While waiting in the student pickup line at Margo's school, Gru took a deep breath, checked his watch, and turned around to check on Gru Jr. in the car seat. The baby was calm now and peacefully sucking on his binky.

"Okay, Daddy is *officially* exhausted," Gru said out loud.

Next to Gru Jr., the back seat was filled with balloons. Gru gave him a stuffed animal and tapped the balloons. He hoped that was enough to distract the baby for a moment.

"Alright. A little bit of me time," Gru said, fairly sure that the baby couldn't possibly want anything else. He grabbed his warm beverage from the cup holder and closed his eyes. This was the closest thing he'd get to relaxation that day, and he wanted to relish it.

He took a sip.

Then . . . **POP!** One of the balloons in the back popped, which startled Gru. He threw the cup up in the air, and the drink spilled all over his head and face. In the rearview mirror, Gru could see Jr. sucking his pacifier and looking away, seemingly unbothered.

Gru frowned. So the drink was a bust. That must have been a faulty balloon. Maybe a banana would provide some bliss? He pulled a banana out from a bag of groceries and peeled it, but then . . .

POP! Gru was startled again and yelled. This time, he smashed the banana onto his nose.

Gru sighed and removed the peel, banana still on his nose. He spun around to see Gru Jr. innocently sucking on his pacifier. Little did Gru know, in actuality, the baby had a safety pin and flicked it around like a switchblade, popping balloons. But every time Gru looked back at the baby, the safety pin was tucked away, and the baby was just looking at him innocently.

Then Margo climbed into the car, completely covered in glitter.

"Someone filled my locker with glitter. Teenagers are the *worst*," Margo explained before Gru even thought to ask what had happened.

She grabbed her seat belt and took her first look of the afternoon at Gru. He still had remnants of banana on his nose, and he looked downright miserable.

"Yeah, babies are no picnic either," Gru said.

Gru wiped the banana off his face and shifted the minivan back into gear. They had just made it out of the school parking lot when—

POP! Another busted balloon.

The noise startled Gru so badly *yet again* that he swerved onto the sidewalk and plowed right into one of the school's signs.

That night, Phil and Ron snuck up to Ralph, who was sound asleep in his vending machine.

The Minions were too short to reach the vending machine's operating system, so Ron climbed on Phil's head, put a coin in the machine, and pressed some buttons. Success!

PLOP! A can of soda dropped down. It bonked Ralph on the head as it exited the machine.

Bwahaha! Phil and Ron laughed.

Ron retrieved the soda can. He shook it, popped the tab with his mouth, and tossed it back into the vending machine.

"Fire in de bowl!" Ron shouted.

The can erupted inside the vending machine, pressing Ralph against the glass and filling up the entirety of the machine with soda spray.

Phil and Ron laughed and walked away.

Later that night, Gru was taking out the trash when he was interrupted by an ominous voice.

"Hello, Gru."

"Hello—wah! Hey, what, what the—?"

Gru looked all around him, but couldn't see anyone. Then Poppy's face appeared, illuminated by the light of her cell phone.

"Oh, hello, Poppy. Did you say something?" Gru asked, trying his best to sound cheery but clearly quite taken aback. Poppy had definitely said *Gru*. How? Why? She couldn't know that name. No one could know that! "My name's Chet, by the way. Chet Cunningham." He chuckled unconvincingly. "Gru. What—what does that even mean?"

"It means you're bad at lying," Poppy said to him.

Trying to take back control of the conversation, Gru interjected. "Hey, that's not nice. Ever hear of respecting your elders?"

"I don't respect boomers. I just mock them."

"Ah, ha, ha," Gru replied. "Is that, like, a job you read about on the web?"

"Wow, 'the web'? How old are you?" Poppy asked.

"Well, old enough to know that you're a rotten little— uh . . ." Gru looked around. Where had Poppy gone?

Poppy emerged behind him, which startled him further.

"You better watch yourself!" Poppy said.

Poppy held up her phone and showed Gru several old photos of him in full villain mode.

"You used to be a master villain," she added.

"Pwah! That's not me," Gru replied nervously. "I don't even see a resemblance. Clearly, you have the wrong guy, as I sell . . ." What *did* he sell again? "Solar panels!"

Poppy raised her eyebrow. "Oh, don't worry. I'm not gonna expose you . . . because you're gonna help me pull a heist. We start planning tomorrow."

"*YOU* want to pull a heist?" Gru asked. Who was this girl? "Listen, kid, I'm not going to—"

"No, YOU listen, old man!" Poppy poked him with her finger. "I promise, you do *not* want to cross me!"

"Okay, uh, alright. But tomorrow is not really good timing," Gru said to her.

"Bummer for you because this is happening. Unless you want the whole world to know exactly who you are, *Gru . . .*"

Poppy swung herself over the fence and into her backyard. Then her face dipped behind the fence, and she was gone.

Gru was stunned and speechless. He nervously muttered to himself, "She is terrifying," but he knew Poppy was right. He'd have to listen to what she said, no matter how badly he didn't want to.

CHAPTER 9

Meanwhile, at the AVL headquarters, a Minion was sitting at a table in the break room. He had a warm drink in a mug that read "I HEART AVL." The Minion was adding a *ton* of sugar cubes to the drink. The more sugar cubes, the better.

"Look-a!" said another Minion, getting the sugar-cube Minion's attention.

It worked. The Minion looked over to see Mega Minion Tim squeezing through the shut door of the break room and opening it. Then the rest of the Mega Minions followed, acting like rock stars. They were strutting, flexing, and showing off their newfound enhanced powers.

The other Minions cheered. After all, this display of power was impressive! Mega Tim stretched his arm to give high fives down a table, but his arm smacked the Minions in the face as it retracted back toward him.

SLAP, SLAP, SLAP, SLAP!

A regular Minion holding pom-poms and wearing an "I HEART MEGA DAVE" T-shirt cheered as the Mega Minions entered the break room. Mega Dave gave him a forceful high five that sent the regular Minion flying, but Mega Gus caught him before disaster struck. The Minion was grateful and motioned to snap a cool selfie, but Mega Gus dropped him while they were trying to coordinate a pose.

CRAAAASH! The force caused the Minion to slam into the microwave below.

There *had* been a Minion about to use the microwave. He was going to reheat his drink, because it had now grown cold. The Minion stared at the broken microwave. Now he'd never get his warm drink.

Mega Mel offered to help heat his drink. But his laser shot right through the coffee cup and out of the AVL building, through the ground and cut an igloo in half on the other side of the entire globe, and out into space, slicing a satellite in half.

Mega Tim used Mega Jerry's rock body to stop Mega Mel's laser, but not before Mega Jerry's head was on fire.

A regular Minion burst into laughter. Another started to roast a hot dog over the fire on Mega Jerry's head. Then the Minions used Mega Jerry's rock mouth as a bottle opener.

FSSSST! The crowd of Minions exploded with laughter. Some rock stars the Mega Minions were.

In the midst of it all, Silas entered the break room and witnessed the Minions' destruction.

"Alright, alright! Settle down, settle down," he called out. He turned to the Mega Minions. "It's time to get you out for some real-world training."

CHAPTER 10

The next morning, Perry and his wife walked toward their car. They were talking about something terribly boring when Gru called out to them. He and Lucy were outside, loading the kids into the minivan. "Morning, neighbors!" he hollered. "Still waiting on that invite, Perry!" Gru added, reminding him about the country club.

"Uh," Perry said. He didn't have a response, but his wife brightened beside him. Perry groaned. He knew that look. He tried to stop her, but there was no way. They crossed over to Gru's driveway.

"Hiiiii there! I'm Perry's wife, Patsy," she introduced herself.

"Oh! I'm Blanche, and this is Chet," Lucy replied sweetly.

Patsy smiled back. Then she cut right to the chase. "So I look over here and I see you," she said to Gru, "and, *ha!* I have one of my brilliant ideas. Perry needs a fourth for tennis tomorrow."

"Oh, honey, heh, I don't know. He doesn't seem like much of a tennis guy," Perry tried.

"Much of a tennis guy? I am TOO much of a tennis guy! I'm Mr. Tennis!" Gru shouted. "It's my favorite of all the sports games. With the racket . . . and with the balls . . . so yellow and fuzzy."

Perry groaned. Patsy elbowed him.

"Then we're all set. See you two at the club tomorrow. Toodle-oo!" Then the couple turned away.

Lucy faced Gru.

"You play tennis?" she asked curiously.

"Yes, yes. I play tennis. I'm pretty fantastic, actually . . . Well, at least I was at summer camp."

"Wow, that's great," she said. Then she handed Gru the baby.

As Lucy started up the car, Gru adjusted the baby's hat.

"There you go," Gru told him.

The baby frowned and threw the hat onto the ground.

Gru didn't seem to be making much progress bonding with the baby.

DINK! Seemingly out of nowhere, an origami star hit Gru right on the head. At this, Gru Jr. giggled.

"Huh?" Gru mused. He picked up the origami star and spotted none other than Poppy in her bedroom window; she was clearly the culprit. She lowered the blinds.

Gru unfolded the paper. Inside the folds was an elaborate invitation with an image of Poppy in front of a tree house. A flap read: "MEET ME IN MY TREE HOUSE." Another flap read: "OR ELSE."

Gru sighed.

Seriously, what choice did he have here?

VROOOOM! Valentina was piloting the massive roach ship while Maxime searched the ground with a periscope. He was determined to find where Gru and his family were hiding.

Behind Maxime, there was a huge photograph of Gru displayed on the monitor alongside a map of the city, scanning for his location. Maxime was going to find Gru no matter what, he promised himself.

"Gru! You can't hide from me, Gru!" Maxime sung.

Valentina stretched her back as she adjusted herself in the pilot's seat.

"My back is killing me! How long is this going to take?" she asked Maxime.

"It will take as long as it takes! Mark my words . . . Gru will not win!" Maxime replied. Then he slammed the periscope shut. "Zis won't be like the ninth-grade talent show."

"Ay, again with this?" Valentina asked.

"Yes, *again!*" Maxime snapped back. "It was a pivotal moment! Why can't you indulge me?!"

Valentina groaned. She could protest, but it was no use. Maxime was going to start again, whether she wanted to hear it or not.

"It was the night of the big show. I had practiced for weeks, perfecting a number that would blow my classmates away! I was about to go on when . . . I heard it!"

Gru, as a ninth grader, had decided to perform the same number as Maxime in the talent show.

"He ruined everything! I couldn't go on after him. I would have looked like a fool. Like I was copying *HIM*!"

Valentina sighed. "Maybe it was just a coincidence. That was a very popular song."

"Oh, no, no, no, no!" Maxime cut in. "He *knew*! He did it on purpose! He reveled in humiliating me."

Just then, a red light flashed in the cockpit, and an alarm sounded. Maxime frowned.

"Huh? What now?" he asked.

"Ugh. We're low on fuel," replied Valentina.

"It's always something. Look. I can never focus on just being evil. Ugh, okay, pull over!" Maxime commanded.

FSSSSHHHHH! Moments later, the massive roach ship touched down at a tiny gas station. The doors opened, and Maxime and Valentina stepped out. She walked the nozzle toward the ship while Maxime went to pay at the pump.

Maxime looked over at the screen.

"Okay, let's see. Regular unleaded. Ooo! Wow, it is expensive, no? Okay. Insert card and remove rapidly."

Maxime inserted his credit card into a slot and pulled it back out. The screen buzzed. Then Maxime frowned as he looked at the screen.

"Card not read?"

He put the card in again and pulled it out. Again it was rejected.

"Oh, come on!"

"Did you pull it out rapidly?" Valentina asked.

"Yes! Yes! Very rapidly!" Maxime replied.

Frustrated, Maxime put the credit card back in and out of the machine several times. No luck. Finally, a pop-up appeared that read: "PLEASE SEE ATTENDANT."

"Ay, get me a slushie," Valentina told Maxime as he marched to the gas station's attached food mart.

Maxime stormed into the food mart and spotted the poor unsuspecting gas station attendant, who, up until now, had been swiping on his phone peacefully.

"Eh, you! Your stupid machine won't read my card!" Maxime hollered.

"Did you remove it rapidly?" asked the attendant.

"Yes!"

"Well, sometimes it's too rapid. You should probably try again."

Maxime growled.

"I don't have time for this!" he hollered.

Maxime slammed his credit card on the counter and grabbed the attendant with his roach claws.

"I'm trying to destroy my archnemesis! Now, give me nine hundred gallons on pump four!"

"Please don't hurt me," the attendant begged.

That gave him an idea. He took the Roachification Ray out from his jacket. Then . . .

ZAP! A bolt of energy hit the attendant and . . . the attendant transformed into a roach monster!

"Oh, look at you! Ha ha. Much better. Now, get me a purple slushie."

The roach monster followed the voice of his new master and scurried over to gather the purple slushie at once.

Maxime beamed, pleased with himself.

"I'm not paying for that, just so you know! So *there*. Ha, ha, ha. I know, I'm *so* bad!" he cackled.

The roach monster handed Maxime the purple slushie and he took it gratis.

CHAPTER 11

Lucy and the girls were at the supermarket, scanning food aisles for staples to keep in the safe house kitchen.

"Hmm. Okay. Why don't you guys pick out a healthy cereal?" Lucy asked them.

Agnes grabbed a colorful box of cereal. She inspected it, but then she seemed to remember something sad, and her face fell.

"This was Lucky's favorite cereal," she lamented. "You don't think he'll forget me, do you?"

"You play with Lucky and dress him up, and you guys have your podcast . . . there is no way in this world he would ever forget his best friend," Lucy told her.

"Thanks, Mom," Agnes said. Then she picked out a cereal with extra marshmallows.

Edith added to the pile with double-frosted choco-clusters.

"Alright, what else do we need?" Lucy asked.

But nothing could have prepared Lucy for the next moment. Her eyes widened. Her heart rate increased. She gasped. Across the grocery store was none other than *Melora*. And Melora's head was wrapped in bandages!

"*Oh no.* Nobody notice, nobody notice," Lucy quietly said out loud. She ducked behind a display and pulled the girls down with her. An orange toppled off, but she caught it and exhaled, successfully drawing no attention their way from Melora—or anyone who might know her. *Phew.*

"What's wrong?" Edith asked.

Lucy carefully put the orange back on display.

"Huh? Oh, nothing. Just, uh . . . oooh! Stretching before we hit the aisles!" Lucy straightened her muscles out and did a big stretch. "Shopping is the number one cause of pulled hamstrings. You probably didn't know that, huh?"

Lucy peeked out and felt relieved. Melora was walking the other way.

"Okay, all stretched. Let's go," she said cheerfully.

She popped up from their hiding place and quickly pushed the cart toward one of the aisles, keeping her eyes locked on Melora, who was shopping. They mustn't cross paths.

"Quickly! Quick, quick, quick, quick!" Lucy urged the girls.

Just when it seemed the coast was clear—

CRASH! Lucy rammed the cart right into a massive pyramid of canned soup.

CLANK-BANK-CRACK-CLANG!

The canned soups all fell over, some of them rolling down the aisles. Now everyone in the store was looking at Lucy . . . including Melora.

Melora's eyes darkened. She dropped her groceries, her gaze never leaving Lucy's face.

"YOU!" Melora shouted. "You did this to me, you fraud!" She pointed at her hair.

Lucy's face fell. Uh-oh. She gathered the girls and took off down the aisle.

"Come on, girls!" she yelled out. "Clean up on aisle nine!" Lucy smiled. She'd kinda always wanted to say that.

But the smile was short-lived. Lucy raced down the aisle as Agnes and Edith followed closely behind her.

"What does that lady want?" Agnes asked her.

Lucy tried to play it off. "Lady? I didn't see a lady."

But when she looked up, there was Melora, rushing toward them!

"Lady!!" Lucy said. She turned to the girls. "Come on, let's go! Faster!"

It was official. The grocery store chase was on. Lucy recklessly drove the shopping cart down the aisles, running from Melora as fast as she could, while simultaneously adding everything the family needed to the cart.

"You're no hairdresser! I'm on to you! Get back here!" Melora called out from one of the aisles.

Lucy rounded some corners and toppled over some bags of flour that were on display toward Melora. Then she purposely threw some sticks of butter on the floor.

Melora powered through the first obstacle no problem, but then she slipped on the butter and began sliding after them out of control.

Lucy needed to think fast. Ahead of them was the freezer section. As Melora slid toward them, Lucy made a beeline to it. Then she turned quickly, pulling the freezer door open in front of her at the very last second.

SLAM! Melora crashed into the freezer, and the freezer door shut behind her.

But if Lucy thought that was it, she should've known better. (Spoiler alert: it wasn't.) Melora punched through the boxes of cookies behind Lucy.

She took off, and the chase was back on.

They zipped, glided, and slid through the grocery store. Lucy threw some cash haphazardly at the cashier for the items, and then quickly headed for the doors, which thankfully opened just in time. The doors shut behind Lucy, Agnes, and Edith and right in Melora's haughty face.

Safe. It was over. They'd won.

Finally, Lucy and the girls had reached the parking lot. The shopping cart came to a stop as it rolled next to their minivan. Just to be super-extra safe, they tossed their items inside, hopped in, and peeled away.

But Melora, still in full chase mode, was hot on their trail, running after them through the parking lot. Lucy safely navigated away from her and out of the lot—and at long last, she could see Melora's silhouette disappearing in the rearview mirror.

"Phew!" Lucy said as her heart rate started to return to normal. "That was a close one. Always a fun time when you go shopping with Mom."

"Best shopping trip ever!" Edith said.

"I feel so alive!" yelled Agnes.

CHAPTER 12

Meanwhile, inside her tree house, Poppy finished putting on her villain outfit. She buckled her belt, put on gloves, lowered goggles onto her eyes, and then placed a pair of goggles onto her cat's face.

Poppy's tree house was decorated with beanbags, a smoothie bar, and neon string lights hanging from the ceiling. Poppy stood on a dance mat in front of a *Kitty 4 Dance* video game, while her cat stood on the adjacent dance pad. It was game time.

At the video game's signal, Poppy and her cat began dancing to the beat. Their feet and paws blurred together in flawless symmetry as they hit every move requested by the game.

"Perfect-o!" the video game's announcer said.

Poppy gave her exhausted cat a high five.

Then Poppy heard a voice whisper-yelling from the outside.

"Poppy? Poppppppy!"

Poppy walked off the dance pad. She approached her tree house monitor and checked the live security camera footage, where she saw Gru (and Gru Jr., strapped to his back) in the backyard. Gru seemed flustered.

"I don't see her, Jr.," Poppy heard Gru mutter to the baby.

Poppy rolled her eyes.

"Look up, genius," she said into her intercom.

Gru's eyes darted upward to the tree house. "How do I get up there?" he asked.

"Use the trampoline."

"Heh?"

On the ground, there was a trampoline that was positioned right under a pair of gymnastic rings, and those rings were dangling from a branch and onto a balcony. Poppy had set up a perfect athletic entrance to her tree house—but Gru didn't exactly consider himself perfectly athletic.

Gru sighed. It was either head into the tree house or have Poppy leak his identity to everyone. "Here we go," he said out loud, and took off toward the trampoline with a running start.

BOUNCE! Gru jumped onto the trampoline with the baby still strapped to his back.

Gru Jr., at least, was enjoying this endeavor. He giggled as they bounced their way up.

Gru swung upside down but then righted himself. In doing so, however, his feet got caught in the pair of gymnastic rings and started painfully doing the splits.

Gru Jr. seemed to like this mishap even more than the initial jump. He laughed and smacked Gru's head.

"Ah! Oh!" Gru said.

At long last, Gru pulled himself onto the balcony of the tree house, Gru Jr. safely in tow. He was a little out of breath, but he'd done it.

Gru looked around Poppy's tree house and took it all in—the beanbags, the smoothie bar, the lights. Poppy's decor wasn't exactly Gru's style, but even he had to admit it looked pretty cool.

Poppy turned around dramatically in her spinning chair.

"It is I, Poppy Prescott, villainess," Poppy announced evilly. "Have a seat, Gru."

Gru sat down on a beanbag chair. The chair wasn't exactly made for someone Gru-shaped, however. He awkwardly sunk deep into it. As he tried to regain his balance and settle in, Poppy's cat meowed and skittered away.

Gru frowned and eyed Poppy.

"Okay, why am I here?" he asked her.

Poppy smiled.

"Because, like you . . . I was born to be bad. And now . . . it's time to discuss . . . our big heist," she said. She stood up and crossed the room.

Gru rolled his eyes.

"Pffft, heist! Please. You're just a child."

Gru managed to pull himself out of the beanbag chair and to his feet. Poppy grabbed a smoothie from her personal smoothie bar.

"All great villains start young. Didn't you steal the crown jewels when you were twelve?" she asked him.

Jr. giggled in delight at hearing his father's past, but Gru covered the baby's ears.

"I was a lot younger than that! And no offense, but you're not me," Gru said.

"Oh, I plan on being a lot better than you," said Poppy. "Check this out." She uncovered a tarp that was draped over something nearby. Gru watched as she did so and raised his eyebrows, impressed. It was an accurate and complete scale model of Lycée Pas Bon School of Villainy.

"Hey, is that my old school?" Gru asked.

"Bingo!" Poppy replied proudly. "Which I have expertly modeled with glue and Popsicle sticks. And it's where WE are going to steal the school mascot!" She held up a model of a honey badger.

"You want to steal LENNY?" Gru gasped.

"Exactly. Lycée Pas Bon has always been my dream school, and this heist will look so great on my villain transcripts."

"That is a terrible idea!" said Gru. "Have you ever seen a honey badger? They are vicious little monsters! They literally eat bees and cobras for breakfast. Honey badger don't care! No way, *no way* am I helping you."

Poppy smirked as she picked up Gru Jr. and booped his nose, which caused him to giggle.

"Well, that's the thing with blackmail," she said. "You kinda have no choice."

CHAPTER 13

The Mega Minions were busy practicing their new powers by helping real people in the city. After all, they were on their way to be heroes. They needed to prove to Silas and the AVL that they could help people in need, and tonight they would do just that as they sought out separate missions.

They were perched on top of a tall skyscraper, and they made their way to the edge of the building. They looked down at the city below as police cars drove by. The skyscraper was high up—it was a *long* way down. They backed away from the edge of the building, just in case.

Mega Dave nudged Mega Tim.

"Tim! Tim! Eh . . . tu le do it! Go, go, go!"

"Porque meo?!" Mega Tim asked.

Reluctantly, Mega Tim stepped toward the edge. The other Mega Minions waited.

BANG! Then they heard a loud noise and a scream. Mega Tim raced back to the group, who all huddled, scared, until Mega Mel broke the huddle.

"Bas enough!" Mega Mel said. Mega Mel was about to deliver an inspiring speech. "Tu le stronga! Tu le forta! Tu le besta!"

The Mega Minions started to catch Mega Mel's vision.

"LES SALAMI!" the Mega Minions shouted.

They threw their hands into the air and cheered. Reinvigorated, Mega Dave was ready to go. He let out a warrior's yell. "AAAAH!"

Then Mega Dave ran off the edge of the building. He landed on the ground and saw a thief steal and run off with a man's backpack.

"No problema!" Mega Dave said to the theft victim. He ripped apart a nearby bike rack and threw a bent metal rod after the thief. But the bent rod soared right past the thief and boomeranged back toward them, accidentally hitting the victim instead, who fell to the ground.

Meanwhile, Mega Gus flew by a window washer when he heard the washer cry for help. It seemed the man's scaffolding had broken, and he'd gotten himself stuck.

"Please, can you help me?!" the window washer begged Mega Gus.

"Oh, sí, sí," replied Mega Gus eagerly. He looked at the window washer's unfinished job and got right to work.

Mega Gus squeegeed the window clean. He sung as he washed. Then Mega Gus dropped the squeegee in the bucket of water, which splashed the window washer in the face. Mega Gus flew away, leaving the window washer still dangling.

"Ciao!" he said.

The window washer watched Mega Gus depart. He sighed. He'd wanted help getting down safely, not washing the window.

Mega Mel saw a cat stuck in a tree.

"Smudge! Smudge, come down!" a woman called to her cat.

Mega Mel knew this was the job for him! He used his goggle-laser to slice off the branch of the tree that the cat was stuck on. It worked and the branch fell to the ground—and so did the cat. Mega Mel caught the cat just in time and rescued him. Wahoo!

The cat's owner ran up to Mega Mel and gave him a kiss on the cheek.

"Thank you, thank you!" she said.

Mega Mel was so happy and surprised by the kiss that his laser went haywire, which blasted off the cat lady's hair, some of the trees in the park, and some of the cat's fur. He zoomed away from the now hairless cat and near-hairless woman.

Mega Tim saw a disaster that needed to be righted when a high-speed train was experiencing a brake malfunction. The conductor was surely going to crash. Mega Tim wasted no time and jumped in to help. He landed in front of the train, attached his arms to the stationary poles, and stretched himself as far as he could to stop the train from advancing.

It worked! The train slowed. The bystanders cheered for Mega Tim, until Mega Tim's super stretchy arms acted like a slingshot and whipped the train backward and into a building.

Mega Tim made a quick exit while the woozy (but still alive) people tried to figure out what happened.

Last, Mega Jerry was patrolling the city when he caught sight of bystanders fleeing from the street. Nearby, a weapon squad inspected the area for explosives.

"Hey, hey! Stoppa stoppa!" Mega Jerry said.

He had a plan. He ate the explosives.

The items detonated safely inside Mega Jerry's rock belly and didn't harm anyone. Everyone cheered, but then—**BLURP!**—they were wiped out when Mega Jerry *mega* burped.

Mega Jerry curled into a rock and quickly rolled himself away.

"Ciao, bellos!" he said.

After their individual tasks were completed, the Mega Minions gathered together, proud of their accomplishments. Except the celebratory moment didn't last. Angry bystanders pointed at them and shouted.

"There they are! Those guys crushed my car!" said one bystander.

"What's their problem?"

"They're ruining everything!"

"I'm sick of superheroes!"

The Mega Minions exchanged confused looks. They thought they were heroes, not menaces!

"Yeah! Let's get 'em!" said the crowd. The angry mob charged at the Mega Minions.

CRACK! SPLAT! CRUNCH! The Mega Minions were in trouble, until . . .

SCREEEEECH! An AVL van pulled up in front of them and the door slid open.

"Get in!" Silas commanded the Mega Minions from inside.

SPLAT! Silas was hit in the face with a projectile tomato, launched by an angry citizen. The Mega Minions didn't miss a beat and jumped in the van. Silas slammed the van door, tomato still dripping from his face, and left the angry mob behind in the dust.

As they made their escape, the Mega Minions sat across from Silas, who shook his head at them, disappointed.

"Gentlemen," Silas said to them. He wiped the tomato off his face. "Our experiment has failed. You are officially going to be retired."

The Mega Minions hung their heads in shame—well, all of the Mega Minions except for Mega Mel, who didn't understand. He pumped his arms.

"Yeah! Retirement!!!" Mega Mel shouted.

Then he saw the other Mega Minions looking sad.

"Ehhh, no?"

He joined them in their sulking.

CHAPTER 14

Gru, Poppy, Gru Jr., and Minions Ron and Phil (who had decided to join them for the heist) boarded a hot-air balloon that was branded with the Prescott Motors logo. Since the school was at the top of a mountain, this was the easiest way for them to get there.

At the sight of the Lycée Pas Bon castle in the distance, Poppy gasped.

"Whoa," she said. "There it is. The castle ... the gargoyles ... I can't believe I'm really here."

The hot-air balloon arrived at Lycée Pas Bon and a rope dropped down.

"Okay, let's get this over with. Ron, hand me my gear," Gru said.

Ron accidentally grabbed a near-identical diaper bag and gave it to Gru instead of the gear bag. Of course, he didn't realize that, or he wouldn't have done it. (Probably.)

"Voilà!" Ron said.

Gru gave him the baby and told him to keep a close eye on Jr.

"Okay!" Ron said.

"If you need anything, I brought his formula, extra diapers, his favorite binky—"

"Come on. Let's go, let's gooooo!" Poppy said, hurrying Gru out of the hot-air balloon.

Poppy rappelled down the rope. Gru followed.

The pair landed on a balcony outside a window on one of the castle's tall towers. Gru removed what he thought was the gear bag from his shoulder and unzipped it.

"Now we cut through the glass with my . . ." He paused and gasped. "DIAPERS?"

Gru looked in the bag and saw that it was filled with diapers, bottles, and bibs.

"What? You've got to be kidding with me!" he said.

The Minions, with the baby strapped to Ron, zipped down the rope and landed on the balcony next to Gru. Then Phil grabbed a bottle from the bag and gave it to the baby, who immediately guzzled it down.

"Hey, guys! Guys. Guys. Guys! Guys! Where is the other bag, with my gear?" Gru shouted at them.

"Ah!" Phil replied. "In le balloon!"

Then Phil and Ron calmly turned and looked up toward the hot-air balloon that was now floating away in the distance with no one to pilot it.

"Ah. Eh. Oops," Phil said. He shrugged. Then he and Ron laughed.

Gru grit his teeth. He could feel himself turning red with frustration.

He tried to compose himself, although the frustration seemed to be spilling out of him. He decided to open the bag and see what he had anyway. He was rummaging through the bag when . . .

"Ah-ha!" he said.

Gru pulled a safety pin out from the bag. Then he expertly used its sharp edge to cut a hole in the glass window.

When that was done, Gru pulled out two full-sized bottles, removed the bottle nipples, and gave the drinks to Phil, who chugged them.

Gru used the bottle nipples as suction cups to gently remove the glass without breaking it.

Poppy clapped, impressed.

Gru smirked.

"Easy peasy," he said.

The crew made their way inside the castle. They started descending a ladder made of baby blankets and into the second floor of the castle. It was seamless. Well, almost seamless.

CREEEEAK! They heard a door open and looked down to see a creepy-looking janitor entering the hall.

"That's Mr. Friendly," Gru whispered.

Mr. Friendly muttered to himself. He was anything but friendly.

The crew waited for him to shuffle by. While doing so, Phil accidentally bumped into Ron and the baby. The baby's pacifier popped out of his mouth and fell.

It was just about to hit Mr. Friendly smack-dab in the nose when a hand reached down and caught it.

Poppy exhaled in relief. Gru was dangling over the old janitor's head. It was his hand that had come to their rescue!

Mr. Friendly lumbered out of the hall.

Once the coast was clear and Mr. Friendly was gone, the group jumped down and took off running in the opposite direction. Ron was the last one to land with the baby on his back. He used Phil as a crash pad.

Gru led the crew down a hallway that was lined with photos, trophies, awards, and various other accolades.

Poppy smiled, taking it all in.

"That's Docto Destructo. He was just a kid!" Poppy said, and pointed to a framed photograph on the wall. "And there's Killer Driller's original helmet." She gestured to a drill-shaped helmet on display.

"Come on, stay focused," Gru told her.

The gang peered around a corner and spotted a security camera.

Thankfully, the security guard monitoring that particular camera didn't care about his job; he was reading a book.

Gru snapped and gestured at Phil.

"Diaper," he commanded.

Phil pulled a diaper out of the bag. Then he and Ron sling-shot the diaper up and onto the security camera so that it completely covered the camera's view, just in case the guard got bored during chapter sixteen.

The security guard reading the book stirred, but otherwise didn't notice.

The group continued to make their way through the school. Finally, they reached their destination: Principal Ubelschlecht's office.

The only problem? The door was locked.

Poppy pulled out a bobby pin from her hair and held it up.

"How 'bout this?" she asked, smiling.

"Nice," Gru replied, impressed.

Poppy beamed. She put the pin in the keyhole, and . . . **CLICK!** The door unlocked.

"Yes!" Poppy cheered.

Poppy hastily moved toward the opening, but Gru put out an arm and stopped her.

"Wait! No, no, no, no, no," he said to her. Then he called to Phil, "Baby powder."

Phil dutifully unzipped the diaper bag and handed Gru a bottle of baby powder. Gru uncapped it and then blew a cloud of powder just inside the office door, which revealed . . . a network of previously undetectable laser tripwires!

"Whoa," Poppy breathed.

Gru smirked. "You know, the most important part of a heist is being constantly aware of potential danger—" But just then he was interrupted by the Minions yelling and pointing.

Gru turned to see what they were frantically hollering about.

It was Jr.! He'd crawled through the doorway and underneath laser beams. He was totally out of Gru's reach—and in imminent danger.

"No, Jr.! Jr., come back here!" Gru shouted.

The baby looked back but didn't listen. He crawled deeper into the principal's office.

"So what's your plan now?" Poppy asked Gru.

"I am dealing with it!" he replied.

The baby crawled onto Principal Ubelschlecht's desk and giggled. He picked up a pen and played with it.

"Oohhhh! Don't touch anything! No, no, no, no, no, no, no, no, n—"

Too late. Gru Jr. pressed a bust of Principal Ubelschlecht. **ZRRRRT!** All the laser tripwires turned off.

Did Jr. really unlock the lasers for them? Gru and Poppy celebrated.

ZRRRRRRT! Nope. The lasers turned back on. Gru and Poppy sighed.

The baby giggled. He turned the lasers off again.

On.

Off.

On.

"Aw, he's having fun," Poppy said.

"Eh, too much fun," replied Gru.

Not one to miss out on the opportunity for "too much fun," Phil stuck his arm in and out of the lasers. Ron chastised him.

"Please, Jr., Daddy needs to steal a honey badger!" Gru begged the baby.

At this, the baby finally turned the lasers off—for good—and crawled away.

Phew. Gru, Poppy, and the Minions entered Principal Ubelschlecht's office.

"Woo, okay. I know they keep Lenny here at night," said Gru. He scanned the office for any sign of the badger. "And if memory serves . . . there is a hidden switch around here somewhere." He noticed a trophy made in Lenny's image and lit up. "Ah *ha!*"

Gru pulled on the trophy's tail.

CLICK! He activated the trigger.

"Yes!" Gru exclaimed.

The ceiling opened up, and a large cage dropped down. Poppy gasped.

"Oooh!" said the Minions.

Inside the cage was Lenny the honey badger, snoozing peacefully. If he stayed asleep, their heist was golden.

Gru took a tranquilizer dart from a case labeled "IN CASE OF HONEY BADGER EMERGENCY."

The Anti-Villain League (AVL) is an ultra-secret organization dedicated to fighting crime on a global scale.

When Gru and his family assume new identities, the Minions are brought to the AVL headquarters.

Silas Ramsbottom selects five of them to receive a super-serum that will help them go head-to-head with Maxime Le Mal.

Some of the Minions find themselves with new identities of their own.

The other Minions get to enjoy all the amenities that the AVL headquarters has to offer.

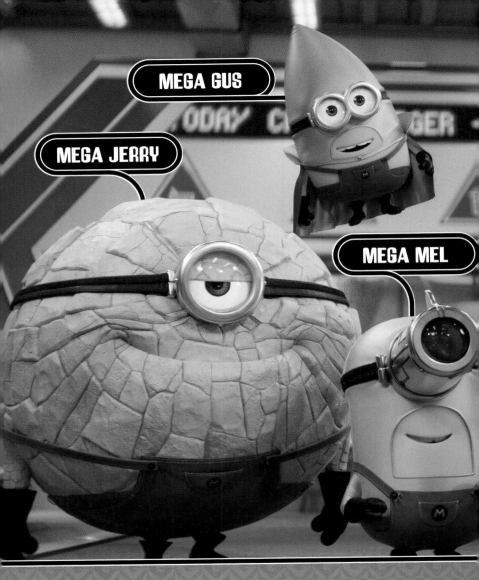

MEGA GUS

MEGA JERRY

MEGA MEL

After the AVL's super-serum . . .

SLAM! Mega Dave becomes super strong.

STREEEEETCH! Mega Tim can stretch like elastic.

ZOOP! Mega Mel can shoot a laser beam from his eye.
SMASH! Mega Jerry has a tough, uncrushable rock body.
ZIP! Mega Gus can fly.

Together they are . . . the **Mega Minions!**

Of course, Mega Minions have *mega* fans.

Lots of fans.

The Mega Minions are still getting the hang of their new powers.

When Silas witnessed the destruction at AVL, he had an idea. "It's time to get you out for some real-world training," he said.

He dropped his voice down to a whisper and explained the plan to Poppy. "I'll hit him with this. Once he's knocked out, we'll open the cage. That fuzzy demon will sleep like a baby the whole—"

CREEEEE! Gru Jr. unlatched the honey badger's door and flung it wide open!

Gru yelped, frozen in fear, when he noticed that somehow, Lenny was still asleep inside.

RAAAAAWRRR! Never mind! Lenny leapt out of the cage. Gru yelled and dropped the tranquilizer dart, which soared through the air and stuck in his right butt cheek.

THUNK!

"AAAAH!" Gru screamed. He rolled over in terror, which inadvertently pushed the tranquilizer serum deeper into his leg.

Now Lenny was bouncing off the walls. Gru tried to run away from him, but his tranquilized leg felt like rubber.

The Minions laughed at Gru. Then they ran from Lenny, who was snapping his jaws and swiping his claws at them. He swirled around like he was trying to destroy everything in sight.

The Minions climbed to the top of the chain that held the cage. Lenny snapped at them. Then he started chasing Poppy. She screamed and hid behind Gru.

"GRUUUUU! WHAT DO WE DO?" she hollered at him.

She dove on the desk and accidentally hit a red button on the bust of Principal Ubelschlecht.

ZRRRRT! This triggered the office door to close.

As if that wasn't bad enough, the bust spun around and set off an alarm throughout the castle.

"Oh no," Poppy breathed. "I ruined our heist!"

Deep within the castle, the alarm woke up Principal Ubelschlecht, who had been in her bed. She yanked off her sleep mask, angry.

"Wha—who dares?" she muttered under her breath.

She pulled a lever on her nightstand, which triggered a robotic machine to lift her out of bed and plop her into her wheelchair. Then she wheeled out of the room, determined to weed out the intruder in her office. As she rolled, she ignited rockets on her wheelchair that sent her zooming forward at high speed.

Inside her office, Gru emerged from behind Principal Ubelschlecht's desk. The honey badger wasted no time and popped up right next to him. It was a catfight—no, a honey badger fight!

Gru and Lenny rolled around and thrashed. The brawl stopped only when Lenny crashed into the Minions and sent them flying like bowling pins.

Gru Jr. giggled playfully and decided that now was a very good time for a Bahama Medley snack.

Gru nudged his leg, which was still numb. "Wake up!" he hissed. They had to get out of there!

But Gru had more immediate problems. The honey badger had determined its next move—and it was going after the baby.

"NO!" Gru shouted.

Lenny zoomed toward Gru Jr. with terrifying open jaws. **POP!**

Gru had nothing to worry about. The baby stuck his tube of Bahama Medley baby food in the honey badger's mouth and squeezed.

SPLURT!

Lenny froze. He tasted the delicious baby food and happily rolled onto his back. Then he sat back up on his hind legs in front of the baby.

"*What?*" Gru breathed out loud.

Was Lenny . . . begging for *more* Bahama Medley?

Gru Jr. fell on top of Lenny, and the pair cuddled playfully together as he fed him more food. Poppy and the Minions were practically melting at the cuteness of the honey badger and baby becoming instant BFFs.

"Awwww," the Minions said in unison.

The emotions were high, and Phil motioned to kiss Ron, but Ron stopped him with an outstretched arm.

"No. Nope," Ron said.

"Come on. We have to go," Gru urged them.

CLICK! Gru activated a button on the bust, which triggered the office doors to open. Quickly, Gru swept the baby up and fled the office with Poppy, the Minions, and Lenny the honey badger on his heels. Gru stumbled as he ran because his leg was still numb.

"INTRUDERS!!! YOU MESSED WITH THE WRONG PRINCIPAL!" Principal Ubelschlecht's voice hollered down the halls. She and her guards rushed toward Gru and the gang, but they took off in another direction just in the nick of time.

"Here we go! Come on, come on!" Gru urged them.

Gru hopped on top of Phil and began riding him like a horse. They reached a staircase, and the gang slid down the banister and through a large door.

From the top of the stairs, Principal Ubelschlect eyed them. She activated a set of inflated wheels and spikes on her wheelchair.

"Ooh, you won't get away with this!" she threatened. Then she and her guards stormed down the stairs. They broke through the door that Gru and the others were behind, and then all-out chaos ensued.

"AHHHHH!" Principal Ubelschlecht screamed.

Distracted, Poppy accidentally crashed into a safety barrier and barreled off an open ledge. She began to fall . . .

Gru grabbed her hand and pulled her back up.

"Prepare to feel the wrath of Ubelschlecht!" Principal Ubelschlecht rallied.

Thinking fast, Gru pulled out rash cream from the diaper bag.

SQUIRT! He aimed the tube at Principal Ubelschlecht. The diaper rash cream covered her glasses and she rolled over the ledge and hit a wall. Her spiked wheels embedded into the wall. She was stuck.

"Get back here, you! I WANT MY LENNY!" Principal Ubelschlecht wailed, but the gang was already on their way.

Gru, Poppy, the Minions, the baby, and Lenny burst out of the stone castle.

"Follow me," Gru instructed them.

Gru led the gang to a carriage parked nearby. A sign read: RESERVED FOR PRINCIPAL UBELSCHLECHT. That didn't matter. They clambered inside.

Gru turned the keys. The car started with a jolt, but the headlights revealed a new threat—Mr. Friendly was blocking the road up ahead, and he was wielding a janitor's mop like a weapon.

Gru hit a button in the carriage labeled "Flight Mode."

TCHOOOOM! The carriage sprouted wings. Then it raised up and over Mr. Friendly's head and made its way out into the night sky.

The group sighed—this time with relief. In the principal's vehicle, they flew safely back to Mayflower.

Back at the Prescotts' house, Poppy and the Minions hid the carriage in some nearby foliage.

Poppy turned to Gru.

"That was, without a doubt, the coolest night of my life. I can't believe we actually pulled that off," she said.

"Not gonna lie, that *was* pretty fun," Gru agreed.

Ron was holding Lenny, who still had the Bahama Medley baby food tube in his mouth.

"Uh, 'scusa?" Ron asked.

He handed Poppy the honey badger.

"Thanks, Ron," Poppy said. She turned to Gru with a smile. "And thank you . . . for everything. Your secret is safe with me, partner."

"Thanks," he replied.

"Good night!"

With that, Poppy left. Gru was relieved. It had all worked out, somehow.

Gru Jr. cooed in his father's arms, and Gru looked down at his baby.

"Your Dada did pretty good, huh, Jr.?" he asked. He held up a hand for the baby to high-five.

SMACK! The baby actually did it!

Back at the school, Principal Ubelschlecht made a phone call to none other than Maxime Le Mal.

"How's my favorite student?" she barked into the receiver. "You know, I think you and I might be looking for the same person . . . and I know *exactly* where he is."

She cackled. She had a "LENNY TRACKER" and a photo of Gru from her security cameras.

The notification on her monitor went from "SEARCHING" to "FOUND."

On the other end of the phone call, Maxime laughed maniacally.

"Thank you Principal Ubelschlecht!"

He hung up the phone and turned to Valentina, "We got him! To Mayflower!!!"

Valentina smiled and pushed the throttle. The ship blasted through the sky.

CHAPTER 15

In the morning, Gru was still feeling good. All he had to do now was make it through Perry Prescott's tennis game. Easy peasy! Gru opened the closet door, reached in, and grabbed a tennis racket.

"Ah, here we go!" he said.

He practiced swinging it in the living room, but he clearly had no idea what he was doing.

"Okay . . . yeah, yeah! It's all coming back to me!"

(It wasn't.)

The girls giggled at him.

WHACK! He accidentally thwhacked the vending machine, which startled Ralph, who was still inside and reading a book called *The Vending Machine Diet*. Ralph sighed and returned to his book.

"Okay!" Gru readied himself.

"See ya later," Lucy said to the girls.

"Say bye to Mommy and Daddy," Margo told Jr., who was in her arms.

"Have fun at the club!" Edith called out.

"Make good choices!" added Agnes.

"Bye, guys!" said Gru.

Then Gru and Lucy bounded out of the house. They were decked out in their best to blend in at the country club.

After their minivan drove away, the girls heard a voice calling out to them from across the yard.

"Hey, Cunninghams!" the voice boomed.

It was Poppy.

"Um. Hey, Poppy," Margo said sheepishly.

Poppy wasn't her usual monotone self, though. She was all smiles.

"I heard our parents are having a playdate, which is adorable, by the way . . . and I thought you might want to hang out?"

Margo wasn't expecting that, but she also couldn't hide her excitement.

"Oh, yeah, sure! Come on in!"

Margo beamed. She was happy to finally have a friend—someone else in Mayflower she could lean on.

"Let's get this party started, people!" Agnes said.

"I like her," Poppy said, nodding to Agnes. They high-fived.

"Yeah. Most people do," said Edith, and they all high-fived again as they headed into the house.

"Sweet. So, have you guys ever seen a honey badger?" Poppy asked them.

As if on cue, Lenny curiously popped his head out of her backpack.

Gru and Lucy made their way through the country club, taking it all in. There were people playing hardcore tennis all around them. Gru felt nervous. Was he in over his head?

"Whoa, okay, these guys aren't messing around," Gru muttered out loud.

Patsy Prescott spotted them.

"There are my favorite new neighbors!" she hollered. She rushed up to Gru and Lucy and admired their outfits. "I'm lovin' this whole *vibe*. You two look like a couple of pros."

Lucy and Gru laughed.

"Ah, ha ha ha! Yeah, but we're NOT! Ha ha ha," cackled Gru.

"Perry and the boys are waiting for *y'all* on the court," Patsy said to Gru. Then she turned to Lucy. "And *we* are hitting the clubhouse. And *you're* telling me where you got that outfit!"

As Patsy dragged Lucy away, Lucy looked back at her husband, shooting him a supportive glance. *You can do this!*

Gru forced a smile as he watched her go. Who was he kidding? But he had to try. He'd just broken into his former principal's office. He could play a little tennis.

Gru neared the court where Perry and two of his friends were warming up. Perry rolled his eyes, but he still called to him.

"Over here, Chet!"

Gru made his way onto the court, extremely nervous and sweating. He wiped the perspiration off his brow as he pulled out his racket and jogged over to Perry. Then Perry did the introductions.

"Skip, Chip, Chet. Chet, Skip, Chip," he said.

"Hey there, fellas," said Gru.

"How are you doin', Chet?" Chip asked.

"Okay. Haha—ah!"

Perry bounced a ball off Gru's body.

Gru shrugged and laughed. Perry then ran up to the net and then hopped over to the other side of the court next to Skip.

"Chet here is gonna show us fellas how it's done," Perry announced. He prepared his racket. "Right?" But out of Gru's earshot, he whispered to Chip, "I'm gonna SMOKE this guy."

Sweating, Gru prepared to return Perry's serve.

WHOOP! Perry tossed the ball up high.

Gru hid behind his racket. Perry reared back, but—

TWEEEET! A whistle blew. Huh? Who was that referee?

It was a Minion, of course. Phil emerged on the court dressed as a line judge. He was even wearing a visor and whistle around his neck.

Skip looked to Chip, who simply shrugged.

Then Phil marched across the court and toward the judge's seat. He sat down. He blew the whistle again, louder now, and pointed to both sides of the court.

Perry smirked and bounced the ball again.

"Okay, let's do this!" he said.

He threw the ball up to serve, and then—

TWEEEEET! Phil pointed at Perry's foot. He was calling Perry out for having a millimeter of his foot over the line.

"Huh? You've got to be kidding," Perry whined. He tried to play it off, but Phil kept sounding the whistle, so Perry said, "Okay, okay!" and removed his foot. "Better?"

Phil made a gesture that showed he was watching Perry closely.

Perry geared up to serve again.

The ball went straight into the net, which looked a bit higher than usual. Huh?

Gru peeked through the net at the ball. Phil was standing on a step stool, holding the net up high.

Phil whistled again.

Perry approached the judge and shouted, "That doesn't count! And—"

Phil raised a red card. And another. And another.

"Oh, what? You can't just jo—"

Finally, Phil pulled out a giant red card. Then he broke it over Perry's head.

Perry groaned. This game was getting worse and worse.

CHAPTER 16

Back at the safe house, Ron stuffed a gigantic bag of popcorn in the microwave and turned it on. Then . . .

BOOM! Popcorn exploded behind the kitchen door.

Edith walked over to the kitchen with a bowl and opened the door. When she opened it, she saw a solid wall of popcorn. There was Ron, encased in the middle of it. He was woozy and he spit some popcorn out of his mouth.

"Cool!" Edith said.

She scooped some popcorn from the massive wall and closed the door behind her as she left, leaving Ron where he was.

Then she walked into the family room, where Margo, Poppy, Agnes, and Gru Jr. were playing with Lenny.

Lenny immediately lunged for the popcorn. Edith held it out of reach, but some popped kernels fell onto Jr.'s walker who fed it to Lenny.

"This is the weirdest dog ever," Agnes remarked as Gru Jr. fed Lenny some popcorn.

DING DONG! The doorbell chimed.

"I'll get it," Agnes said. She left the room.

Agnes approached the front door. Her tiny hand grabbed the door handle and she opened it.

"Well, hello, little one. Is your daddy home?" the woman on the other side of the door asked. Agnes couldn't have known it, but it was Principal Ubelschlecht!

"Sorry. I'm not supposed to talk to strangers," Agnes replied.

"Oh, I'm not a stranger," the principal replied.

"Well, you look strange to me."

Principal Ubelschlecht frowned. Then Agnes heard Margo's voice call from inside.

"Who is it?" Margo asked.

"I don't know," Agnes called back. She whisper-yelled, "But she's old and smells like pickles."

As if he had just gotten a whiff of the pickle smell in the family room, Lenny sat up. He sniffed. Then he bounded under a piece of furniture and *whimpered.*

"Okay, I'm coming," Margo said, and walked toward the door.

Poppy looked through the window and saw Principal Ubelschlecht. Her eyes went wide. Unlike Agnes or Margo, she knew *exactly* who that was . . . and what she was there for.

"Oh no! Um," Poppy said. She scooped Lenny up. "I'll be right back!" Then she ran out the back with Lenny.

Meanwhile, out front, Margo arrived at the door.

"Can I help you?" Margo asked the old woman.

"Well, I hope so. I'm an old friend of Gru's," said Principal Ubelschlecht.

Gru's? Margo and Agnes exchanged a look. This woman wasn't supposed to know that name!

"Well, he's not here, so . . ."

"Oh, that's alright. I'll wait," replied Principal Ubelschlecht.

Then she wheeled past the girls and invited herself inside.

Mayday. Mayday!

Back on the court, Perry was growing increasingly frustrated. His hair was disheveled, and his face was dripping with sweat. Phil rolled the ball machine over to pelt him with balls, over and over again.

Gru laughed. Behind him, Skip dropped his racket and ran away.

"Whenever you're ready, Perry!" Gru chided him. He was having some fun now, but it wouldn't last long.

DING! Gru opened up his messages on his phone to see multiple notifications from Margo. She wrote that someone was looking for him. For *Gru*.

Gru gasped. *Oh no.*

Meanwhile, Patsy and Lucy were sipping their drinks outside the lavish clubhouse.

"... Needless to say, Perry and I are no longer welcome on the island of Oahu. Ha, ha! True story!" Patsy said, laughing.

Lucy chuckled awkwardly. She couldn't relate to a single thing that Patsy had said.

Gru slid into the clubhouse, nearly out of breath.

"Honey!" he called out.

"Oh, thank goodness," Lucy said.

"It's the children—we have to go. *Now!*"

Lucy chugged her drink quickly and then finished off Patsy's.

"Thanks. Bye!" she said to her neighbor. Then the pair made a beeline for their minivan in the parking lot. Lucy wanted to know what constituted such an emergency, but she wasn't exactly complaining about being free of Patsy.

"Our cover's blown," Gru told her as they bolted across the lot.

"What?!" Lucy yelped.

"Call Silas!"

Lucy pressed a button on the side of her smartwatch. Immediately, the screen flashed with the AVL logo.

The signal reached the AVL headquarters, down the satellite dish, through the various AVL cubicles and hallways that were now filled with Minions goofing off and partying, and all the way to Silas Ramsbottom, who had a napkin tucked into his collar. He was just about to bite into a large sandwich when he caught wind of the signal.

EEERT-EEERT-EEEERT!

It was coming from Lucy. That could only mean one thing.

"Gru's been compromised," Silas said. He set his sandwich aside and sent out an emergency signal . . .

but it wasn't for the other AVL agents. "This is an emergency, people! Retirement is officially over—ASSEMBLE THE MEGA MINIONS!"

Mega Gus, who *had* been enjoying a tropical drink at the beach, was feeding a large flock of seagulls. But when the AVL logo on his suit beeped and flashed red, he happily leapt up and flew off. The seagulls trailed after him.

Mega Mel, who *had* been blasting holes in wheels of cheese high in the Swiss Alps, lit up when he saw his own communicator go off. He wanted a second chance. He wanted to be a hero. Mega Mel jumped to his feet, ready for action, and excitedly knocked the large wheels of cheese down the mountain, where he melted them with his laser. Then, naturally, he skied down the melted cheese and headed to save Gru.

Mega Dave, wearing a beekeeper hat, opened a beehive that was full of bees. The bees flew out of the box and formed the shape of a heart . . . just when Mega Dave's communicator went off. This excited Mega Dave. He ran off, followed by his loyal bees.

Mega Tim *had* been lassoing a bull on a dude ranch when his communicator sounded. Both Mega Tim and the bull looked at the communicator and then at each other. Mega Tim cheered—he was being called back into action! He hopped onto a bull, rode toward the signal, and all of the other bulls followed his lead.

Last was Mega Jerry. Mega Jerry *had* been risking it all and winning big at a casino when his communicator started beeping. Even though the machine was paying out gold coins, he started to leave. But he couldn't resist and doubled-back for a big mouthful of coins before speeding off.

CHAPTER 17

The girls sat on the sofa across from Principal Ubelschlecht, watching her. There was an awkward silence as the baby played in a rolling walker beside them. Principal Ubelschlecht stirred her tea.

"So. Your father has been naughty. *Very* naughty," Principal Ubelschlecht said at last. "He took something of mine that I *desperately* want back!"

There was fire in her eyes. And then . . .

BAM!

Gru and Lucy burst through the door.

"Principal Ubelschlecht?!" Gru questioned, surprised to see her and not Maxime.

Principal Ubelschlecht rolled toward Gru.

"Oooh, I know you took my Lenny! Now hand him over!" she demanded. She whipped out a ruler and thwacked Gru with it.

"Ah! Ow! That's, heh, actually a very funny story," Gru began.

"Zip it! I don't want to hear your excuses. I'm here to teach you a lesson," Principal Ubelschlecht replied. She swung her ruler around like a weapon. "Let's go, tough guy!" She stuck the ruler in Gru's face. Gru took it and dropped it on the ground. He was trying not to laugh.

"Okay, I'm not going to fight an old lady," he said.

"Oh yeah? Well, I'm gonna give you a whoopin' for the history books!" Principal Ubelschlecht shouted.

ZZZZT! She pressed a button and a robotic arm emerged from her wheelchair with a metal claw that moved toward Gru. The robotic hand snapped and lunged at him.

"Whoa," Gru said.

Gru ducked and dove out of the way. He barely escaped the powerful robo-hand when—

SNAP! SNAP! It grabbed Gru's feet.

"Take that!" Principal Ubelschlecht shouted. She pressed a different button and another robotic arm grabbed Gru's arm. Then it tossed Gru across the room, finally slamming him into Ralph's vending machine.

Ralph ate some popcorn and cheered.

Lucy grabbed the baby, who was still in his rolling walker, and lunged for the girls in order to protect them. She pulled them all under a table and away from danger.

"Everyone, get down!" Lucy commanded.

Once the kids were safe, Lucy jumped into the fight. She grabbed the back of Principal Ubelschlecht's wheelchair and wrestled it to the ground.

Unbeknownst to Gru, there was more trouble on the way. Maxime Le Mal's roach ship soared overhead, and it was heading into Mayflower.

The girls and the Minions saw Gru and Lucy in the fight and decided to join in. It was like their karate class.

"Stop it!" Margo commanded the principal.

"Let him go!" echoed Edith.

They grabbed plates, cups, and whatever else they could find and hurled the items at Principal Ubelschlecht.

Gru Jr. watched as his family worked together. He may have been only a baby, but he wanted in on the action. He charged forward like a tiny warrior. But as the baby moved forward, Principal Ubelschlecht backed up, and he rammed into the back of her wheelchair.

BOING! The baby bounced off and went spinning across the room—and out the door.

Also out the door was the roach ship, parked on the safe house's lawn. Maxime laughed.

"Now we have to get in there and find that baby—" he started to say, but was interrupted by the commotion of Jr. rolling out of the front door.

Maxime and Valentina shared a look. Could their luck really be this good?

"Oh! Jackpot, huh?" Maxime said.

"Ay, Maxime! This is too easy!" added Valentina.

Gru Jr. looked up at the villains nervously. Maxime reached for the baby.

"Oh, come here little bébé . . . come to Maxime. Yes, coochie-coochie—"

He was about to grab the baby when . . .

CHOMP! Gru Jr. bit down on the villain's finger.

"Ah!" Maxime yelped. He pulled his hand away and cradled his throbbing finger in his other hand.

The baby bounded back for the front door, rolling as fast as he could, but Valentina noticed. She grabbed him out of his walker.

"Gotcha!" Valentina said.

The empty walker rolled back inside the house.

As the fight continued inside, Lucy thought fast and broke a lamp. She used the lamp's electricity to short out the wheelchair, which caused the robotic arm to short-circuit and drop Gru.

Ah. Lucy breathed a sigh of sweet relief. But then a horrific feeling came over her. Where was the baby?!

"Ah!" Gru gasped.

Lucy turned to look at what Gru was seeing.

It was Gru Jr.

Or rather, *not* Gru Jr. His empty walker was at the open front door, and she could hear him crying in the distance.

Principal Ubelschlecht took this moment to strike back—she grabbed Lucy with the robotic hand and held her up in the air.

"Lucy!" Gru called after his wife.

"Go after the baby!" Lucy instructed him.

Gru nodded and ran off.

CHAPTER 18

"**M**axime!" Gru bellowed, confirming the worst: not only had Maxime found the AVL safe house, but he had *also* taken Gru's baby.

And his roach ship was already blasting off into the sky.

"Say au revoir, Gru! Oh, and don't worry, he will be very happy with his new daddy!" Maxime chuckled, holding up Gru Jr. He turned to the baby. "Right? Look at him? Oh, he *loves* his new daddy!"

Gru Jr. reached out to Gru below.

"Nooooo!" Gru cried. He watched helplessly as the roach ship flew away with his son.

Gru was in total panic. He looked around. He had no idea what to do.

VROOM! Poppy, decked out in her custom villain outfit, pulled up in Principal Ubelschlecht's stolen carriage.

"Get in!" she commanded Gru. "We've got a baby to save."

Gru didn't need to be told twice. He jumped right in.

Poppy slammed the car into gear and hit the accelerator. They peeled out and took to the sky, hot on the roach ship's trail.

Meanwhile, from within the roach ship's cockpit, Valentina had resumed her role as pilot while Maxime held the baby up like an award-winning trout.

"Ahahaha. We got him!" Maxime gloated.

Valentina laughed. Maxime held the baby in front of his face and sneered at him.

"Ah ha, who is ready to become a little roach?" he asked the baby.

Gru Jr. grabbed onto one of Maxime's roach antennae.

"Ow! Let go! Ow, those are very sensitive! Ah! Squirmy little—oh!"

Gru Jr. then got a weird look on his face. He *peed* on the roach ship's dashboard while being held by Maxime.

"Ugh, are you kidding me? You got pee-pee all over my ship!" Maxime complained.

Gru Jr. just giggled.

Maxime turned to his girlfriend. "Valentina! Bring me ze Roachification Ray!" he barked.

"There they are!" Gru said, pointing toward the horizon. The roach ship was below them.

"I'm on it," Poppy said confidently. She pulled a lever. "Here we go!"

The wings of the car shook as they dove toward the roach ship. Poppy struggled to keep the flying car on target, but she managed to steer the car and fly it up beside the ship.

Now Maxime could see Gru and Poppy on his tail.

Poppy pulled another lever, and the flying car got closer to the bottom of Maxime's ship. Gru reached out, trying to grab on to it.

"Take them out!" he commanded Valentina.

Valentina pushed a lever.

One of the ship's legs jerked and hit the car. The impact sent Gru and Poppy flying.

Poppy adjusted her hold on the wheel as best as she could and ultimately managed to regain control of the car—by piloting it upside down!

"Aaaaaah!" Poppy screamed, terrified.

Gru dangled from the back seat. He was holding on for dear life but wanted to be supportive. "You're doing great," he told Poppy.

And she was, all things considered. Poppy flew them toward the roach ship and lowered just enough for Gru to jump down and land on the roof. Then Gru and Poppy exchanged a thumbs-up, Poppy in the car, Gru on the roach ship.

"Go get 'em, partner," Poppy told Gru.

Gru slid down the front of the roach ship. He almost fell but caught himself underneath the ship's windshield and climbed.

Valentina gasped when she saw Gru. She twisted a lever from side to side as the roach ship dove in the air back and forth, attempting to fling him off. But that didn't work. In fact, it made things worse for her. Gru's entire body blocked the windshield.

"Ay! I can't see!" Valentina hollered.

Gru lost his grip and one hand peeled off the windshield, which revealed a skyscraper that was under construction up ahead. Valentina, Maxime, and Gru all saw it at the same time.

"Aaaaaah!" they screamed together.

The roach ship spun out of control.

CRASH! It pummeled into the top of the building, slamming into the steel beams, and sent Gru flying off the ship.

Gru tumbled through the skyscraper construction and across the steel girders as the roach ship came to a complete stop on the roof.

Gru coughed. Somehow, he managed to pull himself to his feet. The roach ship had crashed, but where was his son?

"Jr.!" Gru called out.

Nothing.

Then . . .

Maxime Le Mal emerged from the rubble, a cloud of steam behind him. He laughed diabolically.

"Don't worry, Gru, ze baby is fine! See for yourself!"

Maxime gestured behind him. The baby flew out of the steam—only he wasn't exactly a *baby* anymore. He was a *roach baby*.

Gru gasped.

"And now he belongs to *me*! Isn't that right, *Maxime Jr.*?" Maxime gloated and faced the roach baby.

The baby flew beside Maxime. The pair moved together in perfect sync—the baby was copying Maxime's exact moves and facial expressions. He was Maxime's true mini-me.

"And best of all," Maxime added. "He *hates* you! He really does!"

Maxime and the baby squared their eyes on Gru in unison.

"Let my son go," Gru commanded Maxime.

"Oh, I don't think so. Ze fun is just about to start, eh?"

Valentina, still piloting the roach ship, rose up from the crash. She moved toward Gru and laughed as Gru dodged the ship's advances.

Maxime nudged the baby.

"Look at what a coward your old daddy is, huh? Hahahaha!"

The roach ship crept closer to Gru. Its legs punctured the ground, leaving holes everywhere in its midst.

Valentina chased Gru to the edge of the rooftop.

CRAAAAACK! Cracks began to form in the holes on the roof.

From within the cockpit, Valentina's once gleeful face fell. She knew what was about to happen.

The roof under the roach ship collapsed, and the ship slipped down with it, disappearing into the abyss.

But it wasn't over yet.

On the skyscraper, Maxime marched toward Gru. Gru glared back at him, fire dancing in his eyes.

"You crossed the line, Maxime. Now give me my son!" Gru roared.

Maxime sneered at Gru.

"I told you. He is *my* son now!"

Maxime sharpened his roach pinchers and moved across the steel beam toward Gru. Gru looked around. He had nothing. He grabbed a nearby metal pipe—was that all?

Gru and Maxime fought it out, jousting one another.

Finally, Maxime sliced Gru's metal pipe in half with his lethal pincers. Gru threw the remaining half of the pipe at Maxime, who deflected. Then Maxime laughed again as he came up with a new plan—he cut through the steel beam that was supporting their own weight. Gru was losing his footing as the beam collapsed beneath him.

"Watch your step, Gru! It's a doozy," chastised Maxime. "Too bad you can't fly, eh?"

Maxime and the baby watched in tandem as the beam holding Gru started to tip. And Maxime, still holding the baby, leapt into the air, showing off his ability to fly.

It was now or never for Gru. He charged up the teetering beam and made a heroic leap into the air. He grabbed on to Maxime's foot.

Maxime soared into the air with Gru clinging on.

"Let go!" Maxime hollered and tried to kick Gru off. When that didn't work, he resigned to kicking Gru in the face.

"Oh! Ow! Ah!" Gru yelped. It hurt, but he didn't lose his grip.

Maxime flew the trio through some scaffolding. That, at least, was something Gru could use. He braced his feet on the scaffolding's surface and pulled Maxime back.

Maxime kicked Gru again. This time, his force overtook Gru, who tumbled through the scaffolding.

It was almost the end for Gru, but thankfully, he caught hold of a pole and clung on.

Maxime and the baby approached Gru.

"This ends NOW!" Maxime hollered. Then he said to the baby, "Say goodbye to daddy!"

Gru's face fell. He was beaten, battered, and slipping off the pole. He was losing this fight. This was likely the end. The last time he'd see his son—or anyone.

Gru took a deep breath.

"It's okay, Jr.," Gru said kindly. "Dada loves you."

Gru Jr. looked at Gru. His face twitched as Maxime stomped mercilessly on Gru's fingers.

Then the baby's roachlike eyes, once lifeless, blinked. His focus was on Gru. The light came back into his eyes.

Was he snapping out of Maxime's control?

Gru Jr. narrowed his bright eyes and turned to Maxime. Maxime didn't even know what was happening; he was too invested in the revenge that he sought.

Gru Jr. bit his ear.

Now Maxime knew what was going on.

"Oooh! Ah!" he screamed.

"Get back here," Maxime demanded of the baby, but his commands didn't work anymore. Gru Jr. was in total control of himself as he flew around Maxime like an angry hornet, evading him. He jabbed Maxime in the face.

"Bad baby!" Maxime called.

Gru Jr. was relentless; he kept attacking Maxime's face. Maxime wailed for him to stop, but he wouldn't.

"You are going to feel the wrath of—"

The baby flew up, and . . . Gru appeared behind him!

POW! Gru delivered a mighty punch right in Maxime's face, which sent him soaring through the scaffolding.

"Ahhhhh!" Maxime screamed. He hit several pieces of construction and equipment before landing hard on the street.

Maxime pulled himself to his feet. How was that possible?

"See?" Maxime said. "Not a scratch!"

A cheese wheel rolled by, and the ground shook. Confused, Maxime turned to see the Mega Minions approaching him. With them was a herd of bulls, a swarm of bees, and a flock of seagulls.

Maxime's face fell. They were coming to *squish* him. He ran for it.

But Maxime couldn't run from everything. Mega Mel used his laser to melt a cheese wheel in the air. It fell on Maxime and trapped him inside the gooey cheese. Then a bull ran over him.

"Oh no, oh no, oh no, oh no!" Maxime cried out.

The seagulls pelted him with bird poop.

"Ah, oh, ew, no, eugh!"

There was nothing else Maxime could do—he was the unwitting victim of a bird-poop onslaught. His feet were stuck in the melted cheese. And to make matters even worse for this villain, he was getting swarmed by a whole horde of bees.

Maxime stumbled to stand up.

"Ha. Nice try," he said to Gru. "When I—"

But he didn't finish his thought. Suddenly, he was squished.

Mega Jerry had fallen from the sky and landed on Maxime. His gold coin winnings from the casino splashed everywhere as he did. He snapped a selfie to commemorate the event and laughed.

Gru Jr. flew Gru safely to the ground as a familiar minivan pulled up to the scene. Its doors flew open and revealed Lucy, Ron, Phil, and the girls inside.

Success! The family cheered together. And to make it even better, Poppy flew down in the principal's car. She crashed it into a tree, but hey, she was safe. She rushed over to join the rest of the crew as they gathered themselves.

Then they all joined together in a family hug.

Gru Jr. lit up and wrapped his arms around Gru's neck, finally hugging his dad for the first time.

"Dada," Gru Jr. said out loud.

Gru melted. He could barely hold back his tears as his son hugged him.

"Awww. My boys," Lucy said sweetly.

"You know something? Today has been a real roller coaster of an emotion," Gru said in between tears.

"Gru? Can we go back home now?" Agnes asked.

Gru smiled. They could go home—to their *real* home.

CHAPTER 19

The sun set back at the family's house—their *real* house.

"Alright, there you go!" said a voice. It was none other than Dr. Nefario. He handed Gru Jr. to Lucy. The baby was back to himself—his regular, human, not-roach self.

Lucy smiled and cuddled the baby close.

"Yay! Thanks, Dr. Nefario. Good as new," Lucy said. She kissed Gru Jr.

"No job too small. Or too mad." Dr. Nefario laughed. "Bye then!"

Dr. Nefario left. Now Lucy looked around the family room. Agnes was alone, gazing out a window. She seemed sad. Lucy slid next to her and took her hand.

"Hey. You okay, sweetie?" Lucy asked her.

Agnes sniffled. But before she could say anything else, Gru chimed in from out of the room.

"Agnes! Someone's here to see you!" he called out.

Agnes raced toward the front door and stopped at the entryway of their house. She noticed that Gru had Kyle in a carrier. And ... could it be? Something—or rather, some*one*—peeked from behind Gru's legs. Something goatlike.

"Lucky!" Agnes gasped.

Lucky cocked his head. His eyes widened. Then he ran toward her, bleating the whole time. He absolutely, 100 percent remembered his best friend, just like Lucy had said he would.

Agnes hugged her friend.

"Did you practice your tricks?" she asked him.

Lucky bleated back.

"Okay," Agnes said. "Play dead!"

On cue, Lucky grabbed his heart with his hooves and staggered back and forth, pretending to be dead.

"YAY!" Agnes cheered.

Gru shared a look with Lucy.

"That was ... disturbing," he remarked.

"Yeah, a little bit," said Lucy.

Gru and Lucy watched as Agnes and Lucky ran off together. Then Gru opened Kyle's carrier. He smiled. They'd done it. They were safe.

But there was one more thing Gru needed to take care of.

Gru kissed Lucy and Gru Jr. and then gave him a high five. Before Gru left, the baby reached out for him and said, "Da, da, da!"

At the AVL maximum security prison, Gru sat at a station by a glass wall. He picked up a telephone and spoke into the receiver.

"Ohh. How ya doing, Maxime?" Gru said.

On the other side of the glass wall sat Maxime. That's how maximum his maximum security was.

Maxime was dressed in an orange jumpsuit. He did not look happy.

"What are you doing here, Gru? You came to gloat?" Maxime asked him through the phone.

"Gloat? No, no, no, no. I just—I wanted to get something off my chest," Gru admitted.

Maxime rolled his eyes, which Gru could see through the glass.

"And it concerns the ninth-grade talent show," Gru added. "I *did* steal your song."

Maxime's rage was palpable. "I *KNEW* it! I knew there was no coincidence, you little liar!" Maxime shouted. He was so agitated, a guard had to restrain him behind the glass.

"Well?" Maxime asked when he'd collected himself a bit.

"Well, what?" said Gru.

"Well, where's my apology?"

"Apolo—what are you talking about? I just apologized!" roared Gru.

Maxime wasn't having it. "You just wanted to rub it in! I can't believe you stole my song!"

"Hey, I only did that to get back at you for pantsing me at the homecoming dance," Gru replied.

Now Maxime chuckled.

"Besides, you could have gone on after me. It is not my fault you were afraid. Afraid because I KILLED IT."

"*Afraid?* Ha! I could outsing you any day of the week and all day Sunday," said Maxime.

"Ho, ho, ho. I'd like to see that," replied Gru.

"Any time, any place. You name it, mon ami!"

Gru and Maxime glared at each other. They were nose to nose through the AVL prison glass. Then they both glared at each other, as if they'd had the same idea. Could it be . . . ?

Yup. It was.

Together, they coordinated the AVL prison sing-off. And together, they performed a song—two archnemeses, working together at long last.

EPILOGUE

After the prison sing-off, Gru was back to being Gru. Poppy was now a student at Lycée Pas Bon School of Villainy. And Ralph ... well, Ralph was still in his vending machine at the safe house. Gru and the others had forgotten to take Ralph back with them. Oops.

Ralph woke up and looked around.

"Bello?" Ralph said. "Bellooo?"

When nobody answered, he used his body weight from inside the vending machine to push it across the room and toward the door.

Then, with one strong push, the vending machine glass broke, and Ralph fell out, free at last.

But not for long.

The vending machine tipped over and hit a large red button, which triggered the safe house to go into lockdown mode.

The house quickly shuttered itself tight, and then it disappeared underground.

Ralph sighed.

"Oh strudel," he said.

Oh strudel indeed.